Frances was born in Kent at the beginning of World War II. She has one sister. She married and had two children and has lived in London, Essex, Yorkshire, Athens, Greece, and Berkshire. Was widowed at 47. She began writing at 75 after a stroke.

My thanks always to Kathy Morris who helps me with the electronic order of life and much else. Couldn't do without you Kathy.

FRANCES SPARROW

GRANDMA'S TEETH

AUSTIN MACAULEY PUBLISHERS™

LONDON • CAMBRIDGE • NEW YORK • SHARJAH

A CIP catalogue record for this title is available from the British Library.

ISBN 9781398480926 (Paperback)
ISBN 9781398480933 (ePub e-book)

www.austinmacauley.com

First Published 2023
Austin Macauley Publishers Ltd®
1 Canada Square
Canary Wharf
London
E14 5AA

"Look what I've got, Grandma."

"Where did that come from, Mark?"

"Do you remember I lost a tooth and you told me to put it under my pillow for the fairies?"

"Yes, but you didn't believe me."

"No, I didn't, but I checked with Mum and she said it was worth a try. So, I put it under my pillow last night and this morning the tooth was gone, but this silver coin was there. Am I lucky, Grandma?"

"Yes, you are. It must have been a good, clean tooth the fairies are very particular what they take."

"The fairies, Grandma, I don't believe in them."

"Don't you," said Grandma."When I was a girl, we all believed in them and we gave them all our teeth, but I never got more than six pence. You have got ten pence. In the past we would call that a shilling, which was worth twelve pence."

"Why is the money different now?"

"Well, because the government decided the money should go digital to keep up with other countries."

"So why did we lose two pence?"

"Because all currency had to be in tens, which makes it easier to understand and add up."

"I don't like losing two pence."

"Lots of people complained but we had no choice."

"Do you put your teeth under your pillow now, Grandma?"

"No, Mark, they don't fall out now, the dentist takes them out."

"What does he do with them? He must be very rich with everyone's teeth."

"He throws them away."

"Why doesn't he give them to the fairies? What a waste, doesn't he know?"

"I expect he does but the fairies don't like old teeth."

"Why? What do the fairies do with my teeth, why are they more valuable?"

"I don't know, Mark. I have never met a fairy to ask."

"How can we find out?" said Mark, jumping up and down.

"I don't know, let's think, when you want an answer to a question what do you normally do?"

"Ask you, Mum or Dad."

"But if we don't know the answer to this one. Let's think. I know."

"Do you, Grandma, what can we do?"

"Sometimes if I have a problem, when I say my prayers I ask if I could have the answer when I wake up and, quite often, I wake up with the answer."

"But, Grandma, I don't say my prayers."

"Don't you, oh dear, never mind just ask the question before you go to sleep."

"I will, I will. Will the fairies answer?"

"Perhaps, let's try."

"Grandma."

"Yes."

"Can I go to bed early; I really want the answer."

"So do I, Mark, but if we go too early, we won't sleep. Better to go at normal time."

"It's nearly teatime, there are crumpets for tea."

"Ah, lovely, I do like crumpets dripping with butter," said Mark.

"So do I, but first will you take my book inside while I fold up this chair. It must go inside in case it rains."

"Alright, give it to me. Is Mummy coming home for tea?"

"I don't think so. Put the light on, Mark, it's getting a bit dark."

"It won't come on."

"Oh dear, not another power cut."

"We won't be able to have our crumpets," said Mark.

"Yes, we will. But I shall have to light the fire. While I'm doing that, Mark, will you put the cloth on the table and bring some plates, knives, butter and crumpets and then we will be nearly ready."

"But they won't be ready."

"Patience, Mark."

"You are being mysterious, Grandma."

"Am I, you'll see. Now that's got the fire going, it needs to get hotter. Fetch the toasting fork."

"Where from and what is it?"

"On the wall, beside the fire is a long handled brass fork…see it?"

"You mean this?"

"Yes, that's right. Now bring a crumpet to me. What you do is put the crumpet on the fork then hold it up in front of the fire, which will toast it."

"Grandma you are clever, this is the best tea ever!"

"Well, we won't go hungry will we?"

"No, we won't. I wonder if Mum has done this?"

"Yes, she has."

"She never told me."

"You will be able to tell her when she comes home, let me see your crumpet. I think it's time to turn it over and toast the other side."

"This is great, Grandma, but what about yours?"

"I'll do mine whilst you're eating yours."

"I bet my friends have never done this, it will be something to tell them!"

"There yours is done, let's put it on a plate and butter it. While you eat it, I'll sit on the little stool and do mine. Here you'd better have a tissue, you are dripping butter." Just as Grandma had toasted her crumpet the lights came on."Oh good, now I can have a cup of tea. Do you want some juice, Mark?"

"Yes, please. Can we do this another day?"

"I don't see why not, as long as we can light the fire."

"My friend Geoff doesn't have a fireplace or a chimney, he won't be able to do this, would he?"

"No, he wouldn't, Mark. A lot of houses now are being built without chimneys. I wouldn't like it."

"I am glad we have one, Grandma!"

"It's because this house is older, that we have one. So you can tell. If they don't have a chimney, there is no fireplace and nowhere to toast crumpets or have a fire."

"Don't let us move."

"I wouldn't think of it, Mark. Now make sure you wash all that butter off your fingers and your mouth, clean your teeth and get into bed. I'll come up and we will ask our question and then we will see if we get an answer."

"I'm going. I want to sleep tonight; this has been a very interesting day!"

Mark woke early the next day and lay there trying to grasp what was on his mind-foundations! What did that mean, Grandma will know. He scrambled out of bed and bumped into Grandma coming in."Morning, Mark, did you get an answer?"

"I'm not sure, it doesn't make sense to me. I woke up with one word on my mind: 'foundations'. What does it mean?"

"My word was 'building'."

"It appears that when the fairies are building something new, they need good, strong teeth for the foundations. Did you know that your house is built with a foundation?"

"Is that where the dentist send the teeth? He sells them to a builder, Grandma."

"No, we don't use teeth in our foundations."

"What do we use?"

"Concrete. It's to stop the house moving about or falling down."

"How funny if the houses moved. When I came home from school I wouldn't know where my house was."

"It couldn't go far, could it," said Grandma."There is a house either side of yours, so the only space it has to move would be into the road or the garden." Mark was giggling at the thought of houses moving."There are new houses being built on Sutton Lane. On Saturday I'll take you to see if we can see the foundations."

"Lovely," said Mark.

"In school, the teacher was asking us what we want to be, when we grow up."

"What answer did you give?"

"I said I didn't know. I don't want to drive a train or be a policeman or fireman, scientist or writer. Those were some of the answers."

"Did the teacher help?" asked Grandma.

"Not really, she just listened."

"Oh dear, she should be getting you all to think more deeply. Let's go back to foundations and houses."

"Who builds them, Mark?"

"That's easy, a builder!"

"Who else?"

"The men that carry and lay the bricks."

"Let's go back further, Mark. First of all someone must buy or own the land and want to build on it. Then they need an architect to draw the plans for the house and these must be submitted to the council for planning permission to build. The builder must have a solicitor to make sure he doesn't break any laws, cross any boundaries onto someone else's land and does not impede rights of way over the land. When permission is granted, the builder will need a quantity surveyor to work out the costs of all the materials. What do you think he will need?"

Mark thought."Bricks," he said, staring at his house,"and slates for the roof."

"Yes, but what keeps the bricks together, Mark?"

"Oh, cement."

"Yes, what do you make cement with?"

"I know this, Grandma. I watched Dad lay the patio. He had bags of cement, sand and water."

"What else goes into a house? Wood, doors and floors. The builder is going to need workers who know how to build foundations, read plans, make cement and build walls. Later, he will need electricians, plumbers, plasterers and painters."

"There's lots isn't there, just to build a house?" said Mark.

"Yes, and don't forget his office staff."

"What do they do?"

"There are letters to write, enquiries to be made. Equipment to order and materials have to be on site when needed. Someone has to order them and make sure they come. Then, the accountant has to monitor and pay the bills and keep all the transactions in a ledger. Someone has to work out all the costs and find out how much it is going to cost to build the house. The estate agent will then decide how much he can sell it for. Lots and lots of jobs."

"My teacher doesn't talk like that, Grandma. You had better come to school."

"My school days are long gone, Mark. Now I learn by experience. Watching, reading, listening and thinking. That is what's important."

"Gosh, there's all these jobs to do just to build a house."

"Now think about what you use all of the time and think of the jobs."

"What do you mean, Grandma?"

"Well, the clothes and shoes you use, the books you read, the paper you write on, the china, glass and cutlery you use, the food you eat. Hundreds of jobs to choose from."

"I still don't know what I want to do!"

"Don't worry it will come to you in time. You will get interested in something. Maybe it will start as a hobby."

"We still don't know why they don't want your teeth, Grandma."

"Because they're too old, Mark. To be used in foundations, they must be strong. My teeth are nearly seventy-nine years old, and they have been used a lot. Not as strong as new ones."

"I suppose not. What a pity. Didn't the dentist give you false ones?"

"Yes, he did. The ones you can take out to clean! Yes, I'm lucky aren't I? There are many people in the world who will never see a dentist."

"They are lucky, I wish I didn't, Grandma."

"You wouldn't say that when you get a bad toothache. I shall come for you on Saturday at 10 am, after breakfast, and we will go and see where they are building."

"Thanks, Grandma. Can Mike come? He's my friend and he hasn't got a grandma."

"Of course, he can."

Saturday came at last. Mark was so excited he could hardly sit still."I'm going with Grandma today," he told his mother."Mike is coming with us. We are going to look at house foundations."

"I know," said his mother."Grandma has told me all about it. It should stay fine. I'll do a packed lunch for you, then you can stay out longer."

"All day?" said Mark.

"If you wish, you will have your lunch with you."

Mike arrived. He's got his lunch."What about Grandma?"

"There'll be plenty for you all, enjoy yourselves. Have you got boots; it may be muddy?"

"Yes, Mum, we are ready."

"Good, here's Grandma. Now you be good for her."

"Of course, we will."

"Ready boys, let's get in the car and say goodbye to your mum."

"Bye Mum, come on Mike bring your coat."

Grandma got into the driver's seat and watched the boys scrambling into the back. Mum shut the door for them and waved them off."Is it far, Grandma?"

"Not far," said Grandma. They set off, everyone talking at once. It did not take long, and Grandma parked the car safely off the road. As they were getting out, a voice called out to Grandma saying"Hello". She waved and took us over to the builder.

"Good morning Robert. This is my grandson, Mark, and his friend Mike. They have come to see the new foundations."

"Hello boys, we call them footings. Let's go and see, shall we. Stay this side of me we don't want you falling in. We are waiting for the concrete to arrive."

"Is it coming today?" asked Mike.

"Yes, in about half an hour, not long to wait."

"Is it coming in big trucks with the back going around?" asked Mike.

"Yes, that's right!"

"How do you know that?" said Mark.

"My dad explained it to me last night. I haven't seen one close up," said Mike.

"Are these ditches the footings?" said Mark.

"Yes, that's right."

"They are quite deep aren't they? Grandma, do you know Mr Stephens?"

"Oh yes, Mark, we went to the same school. But Mr Stephens is younger than I am. His mother was one of the teachers."

"Now watch boys, here comes the first delivery."

"Where do you want us to stand Robert? We don't want to get in the way."

"Go over by that tree. Then you will have a good view. Just a moment I need to speak to the driver."

"Mike, I understand now about the back turning around," said Mark.

"The part that is turning is the drum and it must keep the cement moving, so it does not set and go hard in the drum," said Grandma.

"Look it's pointing a shute at the ditch. Look it's pouring out and filling the footings."

"Alright boys!"

"Yes, Mr Stephens!"

"The truck is now going to move near to the next empty footing and fill that as well."

"Will he have enough?" said Mike.

"He should have, but if not, a second one will come."

"When it is hard, is that what the house will sit on?" asked Mark.

"That's right. The bricks will be delivered tomorrow. It won't be long and then we will start building walls!"

"I hope we can come and see that, Gran?"

"I expect we can pay another visit."

"Mr Stephens, will this house have a chimney?" asked Mark.

"It will."

"Good, they will be able to toast crumpets, won't they, Gran?" She laughed and began to explain what Mark meant.

"I've never done that."

"Haven't you Robert, We will have to invite you next time."

"Yes, please."

"Can I come too?" said Mike.

"Of course, you can. It's best in the winter because you have to light the fire."

"Have you got a grandma who can lend you a toasting fork Mike?"

"No, but I will ask Mum."

"This has nearly finished. Just needs a little more and here comes the second load!" Finally, all the footings were filled, and we followed Mr Stephens into a wooden shed to see the plans."These are the plans we work from and this is what an architect does. He has to be very accurate. We don't want a wonky house!"

"That would look really funny," said Mike.

"Not if it fell down," said Grandma.

"I don't think I can show you anything else today and I have some paperwork to do before dark."

"Then we will leave and go home," said Grandma.

"Is it lunchtime?" said Mark.

"It's half past twelve. Shall we go to the park for our lunch boys?"

"Yes, please."

"Thank you, Mr Stephens for having us and explaining everything."

"No trouble at all. I'll see you again as we build the walls."

"Yes, you will," said Grandma, putting a piece of her wrapped cake in his hand.

"Thank you. I'm being spoilt. You can come anytime if there is cake!" They all went to the car and then off to the park.

Mark was bored and was looking for his gran. She always cheered him up and suggested interesting things to do. I expect she's in the garden. Yes, I see her."Found you, Gran."

"Why, was I missing?" said Grandma.

"Only because I couldn't find you."

"Well, if you are looking for me, that means you are at a loose end and do not know what to do!"

"That's right, Gran. It's Sunday, always a boring day."

"Is it, I rather like Sunday, you can relax. Of course, when I was younger everyone went to church."

"Did they, I have never been," said Mark.

"Lots of people don't go now," said Grandma.

"What can we do, Gran?"

"Have you seen the house lately?" asked Gran.

"Yes, last week. I walked past. There was nobody there, but the walls were quite high with spaces for windows and a front door. It's quite quick, isn't it!"

"Oh yes, they'll soon be putting the roof on. Have you seen your friend lately?"

"No, he's been on holiday."

"Where did he go?"

"Wales. Have you been there?"

"Been there, Mark, I was born there."

"Were you, you never said."

"You never asked."

"Is that where you met Grandpa?"

"Yes, he was a postman."

"Now that's interesting, Gran, I never knew that."

"Would you like to start your family tree?"

"Can I. How?" said Mark.

"Quite easily to start with. First, clear the dining room table. Then find a large piece of blank paper and a pen and pencil. Then I will fetch my birth certificate and Grandpa's."

"I have never seen a birth certificate."

"Not even yours?"

"Have I got one, Gran?"

"Of course, everyone has." Mark rushed off to find paper and a pencil and Grandma went upstairs to find her certificates."Is that the largest piece of paper you could find?"

"Yes."

"Well, we will start with it, but later on we will need a much larger piece.

"Now you are going to have to play detective. How far back can you go into the family?"

"Only you and Grandpa."

"But I am here. What do I know? Be a detective." Mark was puzzled."Who are your mum and dad?" asked Grandma.

"Oh, I know that!"

"Of course, you do but what don't you know?"

"I can't think, Gran."

"Here is my birth certificate. What does this tell you?"

"It tells me your name. I didn't know that, as you are Grandma to me!"

"What else?"

"Well, the address where you were born and the date. Oh, and the name of your mum and dad. Gee that's a lot."

"So who's names goes on the top of our piece of paper?"

"Your mum and dad."

"Correct. You put Dad first, then 'M' for married, then my mum's name. She wouldn't have the same name as my dad until she married him. You will want her maiden name which I happen to know was castle. So you should have:

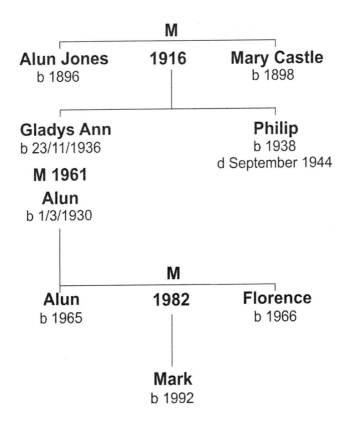

M

Alun Jones   **1916**   **Mary Castle**
b 1896   b 1898

Gladys Ann   **Philip**
b 23/11/1936   b 1938
                  d September 1944
M 1961
Alun
b 1/3/1930

M

Alun   **1982**   **Florence**
b 1965   b 1966

Mark
b 1992

"At the moment, we do not have the date of their marriage. So now, here is my marriage certificate when I married your grandpa." Mark took it and carefully read the details.

"It gives the date and place and both names."

"Yes, so now you can fill in those details onto your sheet. Now can you see what is missing? Your parents can give you some of that information if you ask."

"I am going to ask to see my birth certificate. It's very interesting. There are Mum and Dad now. Thank you, Grandma."

"You are welcome."

Mark was very excited as he showed his mum and dad the family tree and explained that Grandma had helped.

"Can I see my birth certificate please?"

"Well, you have been busy. Of course, you can when you give us a chance to draw breath!"

Later, Mark sat looking at his birth certificate noting all the details.

"Do you remember Aunty Penny, Mark?"

"Yes, Mum. Wasn't she your sister?"

"Yes, she was. She should be on your family tree as well. Her full name was Jennifer Jane Castle."

"I have her. Look there she is, I only knew her as Jenny, but I haven't got you on there yet. You must show me where to put you."

"You will need a bigger piece of paper, as you will have to spread out. Where has your father gone?"

"Will this do?" said his father, bringing in half a roll of wallpaper.

"Well done, love. That will do splendidly thank you!"

"What is the matter, Mark?"

"Dad has taken over."

"Has he?"

"Yes, he's found a computer website and is scribbling like mad."

"Don't worry, Mark."

"I'm not, Mum. I think I will go and look at the house again."

"Alright, see you at teatime."

When Mark got to the house, he saw that the windows were in and someone was putting in the glass.

"Hello, my name is Mark. I've been watching this house being built."

"Yes, Mr Stevens told me about you."

"You put in the glass, so what are you called?"

"I'm a Glazier. This is plain glass, so it is easy to see out of it. There are other types of glass."

"Are there?"

"Have you been into a church and seen stained glass pictures?"

"No, I haven't," said Mark.

"I am taking a course to learn how to make stained glass."

"Are you. Will you work in churches?"

"I don't think so, not many new ones are being built. It can be used in other ways. In doors and lamps for instance."

"I must go to the church and see some. Then I will understand. I will ask Grandma to take me."

"My name is John. Do you know yet what you want to do when you are older?"

"Not yet, I'm busy finding out what is possible."

"Good for you. Well, I had better finish this job before it gets dark. Perhaps, I will see you again?"

"Yes, you might," said Mark.

. . . .

"Grandma, I talked to the Glazier John, today. He was putting glass in the windows of the house. He told me about stained glass in the churches, can we go and see some?"

"Of course, we will. We will go on Saturday."

"That's tomorrow!"

"Yes, it is. There won't be a service on a Saturday."

"Does every church have them?"

"No, Mark, they don't. They are expensive. Usually, you will find that a rich person in the community has paid for them, many years ago. Sometimes, hundreds of years ago."

"So some are old?"

"Yes, very."

The following morning after breakfast, Grandma and Mark set off.

"I think we will start with the cathedral."

"Will that be the biggest?" asked Mark.

"Yes, but not necessarily the best," said Grandma."We will know more as we look. There's plenty of room to park today. Let's see if it is open." They walked towards the big doors which looked tight shut.

"Oh dear," said Mark,"it's shut!"

"No, it's not. See that small door there on the right, I think that is open."

"It's so quiet, Gran. Can we talk?"

"Of course, we can."

There was a cough and a gentleman walked towards them."Good morning. Have you come to see our lovely cathedral?"

"Yes, we have," said Grandma.

"We are interested in the stained glass windows."

"Our lovely windows. Let me show you the way." They followed him and then they saw the windows."We have three here."

"How old are they?" asked Mark.

"Not as old as some but then this cathedral is only two hundred years old."

"I would say that was quite old," said Mark.

"Who paid for them?"

"Sir Jeremy Aickin, in honour of his father, 1727–1805."

"Are any of the family still around?"

"Just one old lady, she is ninety-seven years old. She sometimes comes and looks at the windows."

"Have you spoken to her?" asks Mark.

"Yes, I have."

"Fancy having something like these windows to remember your family by. I have just started our family tree."

"Well son, you never know where it will take you. Quite an adventure!"

"It is exciting, isn't it."

"Yes, I've never done mine. I might look into it."

"When you're ready, just wander around and discover. I shall have to leave you now, nice to have met you."

"Thank you for your help," said Grandma.

"Yes, thank you," said Mark.

They both sat and looked at the colourful windows and Mark, for once, was speechless."Well, Grandma, what do you think?"

"They are beautiful, wonderful colours. They must take hours of work. John is learning to do this. I must speak to him again." After sometime they wandered around, looking for more windows. Only two small windows in niches did they find. Grandma led them back to the three large ones and they decided to go elsewhere to look.

The next church was small, and they had to find the vicar to gain entry. Mark thought he wasn't too happy at being disturbed on his day off. But he did show them the two windows. He told them that they dated back to 1625.

"How old is the church?" Mark asked.

"The oldest part is dated 1100. Then over the years, bits have been built on."

"Is the oldest part Norman?" asked Grandma.

"Yes, that would be the tower," the vicar replied.

"Gosh, I didn't know we had anything as old as that around here."

"You should visit the civic centre. There you can discover lots of old bits."

"Thank you, Vicar, sorry we disturbed you."

"That's alright. It is good to see a youngster interested."

"Can we visit the civic centre, Grandma?"

"Of course, we can, but aren't you hungry?"

"Yes, I am, what time is it?"

"It's twelve o'clock."

"Really?"

"We will see if we can get lunch in the civic centre, although it might be very busy on a Saturday. We shall need the car again." They had put the car in the multi-storey car park and set off to find the civic centre.

There were lots of people shopping, but at last they found what they were looking for. On the big doors was an impressive coat of arms, and inside it was cool and quiet. The lady at the desk sent them up to the first floor. Here in a beautiful room with stained glass windows, another lady came forward to help them."Can I help you?" Grandma explained what they were looking for. She pointed first to the windows.

"We had best start here," she said."These windows were bequeathed to the town in 1760, but previously they had been elsewhere for three-hundred-years."

"Do you know where?" asked Mark.

"Yes, a monastery. The monks removed them and stored them for safe keeping during the reign of Henry VIII. As you know, he ransacked all abbeys, churches, monasteries and nunneries and took all their treasures."

"Why did he do that?" asked Mark.

"It was because of religion. We were all catholics lead by the pope and Henry decided he was not accepting the pope any longer. He wanted to be head of the church."

"I heard some of this at school, but I didn't really understand it."

"You didn't. I'll give you a leaflet which explains it."

"Thank you," said Mark.

"How do all of those tiny pieces of glass stay together?"

"If you look closely, you will see grey around each piece," said the lady."That is lead, which keeps it all together."

"Yes, I see. It must take forever!"

"You definitely have to have patience, a good eye and nimble fingers."

"I don't think I could do it."

"It's like everything else, Mark, you have to learn how, and then you practice. Practice makes perfect!"

"I suppose so, they are lovely."

"These are simple compared to others."

"I think it is time for lunch, Mark, thank the lady."

"Thank you, it's been very interesting."

"You are very welcome. I have enjoyed talking to you, don't forget your leaflet."

"I've got it thank you." He followed Grandma out."That was so interesting. Thank you, Grandma."

"I enjoyed it as well, Mark, let's find something to eat, I'm rather peckish. That means hungry, Mark!"

"Does it, what a funny word! Yes, please, I am hungry too."

"Look there is a place across the road, let's try there. Have a look at the me and you!"

"What's a 'me and you'?" asked Mark.

"A menu which tells you what food they are offering."

"Yes, I understand a menu, but I've never heard it called a 'me and you'."

"That's because you didn't know your granddad. That's what he called it. Anyway let's take a look."

"They have my favourite!" cried Mark.

"I can guess, sausages?"

"Yes, I'll have a sausage sandwich please, Grandma."

"And I will have an omelette. Let's go in and order." And so they did.

Later they went to another church but were disappointed there."Shall we go home, Gran; we have done quite well today."

"Yes, I think so, I can do with a sit down."

As they drove home, Mark said,"I'm going to see if I can find the glazier again, he's learning to make stained glass windows. I would like to know more about it."

"You are really interested then?"

"Yes, I am, Gran, it does appeal to me. It's something different and beautiful as well! When we get home I'm going to tell Mum all about it and then see how far Dad has got on with the family tree. Thank you, Grandma for a most interesting day!"

The next day, being Sunday, Mark sat with his dad and looked at the family tree. It now went back into the seventeen hundred."So many names, I wonder what they all did, Dad?"

"I can't tell you all of them," said Dad,"but there are several butchers and three went to sea. I'm still researching so can't tell you much more yet."

"Yet, all these names belong to our family," said Mark.

"Yes, they do. Interesting, isn't it? I'm not finished yet, so who knows who we might discover. How come you are home today? You are usually off with Grandma, out and about somewhere?"

"We did that yesterday, Dad. We looked at stained glass windows. First, we went to the cathedral. Have you been there?"

"No, I haven't."

"They have three lovely windows, Dad, all paid for by Sir Jeremy Aickin, in honour of his father, who lived from 1727–1805. There is only one old lady left from the family and she often comes to see them. Then we went to the civic centre and saw more that the monks rescued from Henry VIII, who destroyed all the churches, monasteries and nunneries. I was given a leaflet about it."

"It sounds as though you had an interesting day, son."

"Yes, it was, Dad. I'm interested to find out more about these windows."

"You really are interested in this?"

"Yes, I am. I've met someone who is learning how to do it. I would like to find him and have another chat."

"Well, if you need any help, let us know!"

"Thank you, Dad. On Monday, I will go to the house again and see if John's there. If not, I can ask Mr Stephens where I can find him."

....

On Monday, Mark was getting ready to see if he could find John, when Grandma arrived in her little car."Hello, Mark, can I come with you? I would like to meet John."

"Of course, you can, Gran. I was just about to leave. Do you want a cup of tea first?"

"No, Mark, I'm ready, let's go."

"Dad, we're off now. Grandma's with me, see you later."

"Okay, son, enjoy yourselves!"

As they got into the car, Mark started to tell Gran how far back and also what Dad had found, doing the family tree.

"I shall have a look at it. It sounds it's at an interesting stage. Here we are, Mark." They arrived at the site.

"All the windows seem to have their glass in. Let's look around the back," said Mark, leading the way."They're all done, John will not come today!"

"Mark, you have missed one."

"Have I, where?"

"Look over the door."

"Yes, I see. That's where some of the houses have a stained-glass picture. I wonder…can we wait, Grandma?"

"Yes, of course. I'll get the chairs from the car and we can sit and wait."

They made themselves comfortable and they didn't have to wait long before John arrived. "Look there's Robert. He has John with him. What is he carrying, Gran?"

"Hello, Mark, good to see you again. Now you can see the last window going in. This is it. I made it in my course class with the help from my tutor. What do you think?" He carefully unwrapped the window.

"It's a windmill," said Mark.

"That's right."

"Why a windmill Robert?" asked Grandma.

"Don't you remember the old windmill that was here when you were younger?"

"Now you mention it, yes, I do. It was pulled down as it was considered dangerous."

"You're right. I decided to call the road here 'Windmill Crescent' and this house is going to be 'Windmill House'. That's why the window is displaying a Windmill," said Robert.

"Very nice and neat, Robert. How many more houses are to be built?"

"Just three, otherwise there will not be enough land for gardens. And yes, Mark, before you ask, they will have chimneys!"

"In that case, I might consider buying one. I wouldn't want one as big as this, but I must have a garden," mused Grandma.

"In that case Gladys, we had better look at the plans, while John fits the window."

"Now I don't know in which direction to go," said Mark.

"Stay and watch, John, then you can chat and learn," said Grandma.

"Alright, but you will tell me if you decide something."

"Of course, Mark. Now I shall go with Robert and you stay with John."

"John, how long did this window take to do?"

"From the first design to a finished window, about five months."

"That's a long time," said Mark.

"Yes, Mark, you have to have patience to do these."

"John."

"Yes."

"Can I come with you to your class or am I too young?"

"You're never too young to learn a new skill. Do you think you would have the patience, and would your dad pay the fees to buy the materials you will need?"

"I think he will," said Mark."He knows I'm interested to learn. Have you seen the windows in the cathedral, John?"

"Yes, I have. Beautiful, aren't they? Speak to your dad. Here, I have written down some information, the telephone number and the tutor's name. What is the first window you want to make, Mark?"

"One to go over our front door. At present, it is just plain glass."

"You should see if you can find out if there ever was one. It may have been removed. Try the council, they approve all the plans."

"I will. Thank you, John, you have been very helpful."

"I will help where I can. Hope to see you in class, Mark."

"I hope so too. That window looks lovely."

"Thank you, I'm quite pleased with it. Perhaps, Robert might order another for one of the other houses. If we start a trend, other people might want one. More work for us, Mark!"

"Yes, isn't it exciting!"

"So life should be. I shall have to leave now, got another job to go to. I'll just say goodbye to Mr Roberts and your gran."

Mark stood for a moment and then followed John to the shed. He had a lot to think about. Everyone was all smiles when he got there."Mark, I have decided to buy a bungalow on Windmill Crescent, and it will have a chimney, so we can toast crumpets!" said Grandma.

"I shall miss you."

"I won't be that far away. You can visit and still have days out. Besides, the property isn't built yet, we will be able to watch it take shape."

"Oh good," said Mark,"Will you want a stained glass window? John says it took him five months to make the windmill window. So, we must get some designs ready and I'm going to learn how to do it."

"If you make it, Mark, it will be extra special!"

"I hope I can. Life is so busy suddenly."

When they got home, Grandma wanted to see the family tree and have a cup of tea whilst sitting in the garden. Mark went in search of his dad to ask his permission to join the stained window class, and to give him the paper on which John had written all the details. Finally, they both found Dad, made tea and started to pass over their news. Grandma's news of buying a new bungalow was the most surprising, but he was pleased for her and said he would also ring and speak to the tutor to find out the details and then we would see."Good job I have patience," thought Mark.

Grandma spent the afternoon pouring over the family tree."We have to look at the census return, it will give a fuller picture."

"Gran, did this house ever have a name?"

"I don't think so, but we can find out. We will have to visit the council. They will have the original plans and see what we can discover."

"The windmill was a bit of history which has now been captured for the future," said Mark.

"Yes, it is good. I had forgotten the windmill."

"So, can we have another day out, Gran?"

"Yes, Mark. But next time, not on a Saturday. We shall visit during the week. We might have to go several times; it depends how quickly they can find the plans. I'll ring them first to find out what information they will need."

"Will they need the builder's name?"

"Probably. I will ask Robert, he will know."

. . . .

On the following Wednesday, they set off to go to the council offices. Grandma had the name of the builder and had made an appointment to see the planning officer at 10 am. When they arrived, they were shown into the planning officer's office. He introduced himself as John West, then sat and opened the file on his desk."We found the original papers for the property, built by Jack Higgins in 1935. At that time, it only had a number and no name. It was one of five that were to be built. The name of the road had not been decided at that point. I have the original plans if you would like to see them."

"Thank you," said Grandma,"we would like to see them."

He then spread them out on the table."What is this big house here?" asked Grandma.

"That was the old Manor House," said Mr West.

"Is that why the road is called Manor Road?" asked Mark excitedly.

"Yes, I suppose so. The house was taken over during the war and used for training purposes."

"How exciting!" said Mark, sensing a story."How can we find out more?"

"You will have to contact the war office."

"A Manor House. Who lived there and who owned it?"

"I think I know," said Grandma."Do you remember the man who paid for the windows in honour of his father?"

"Yes, Sir Jeremy something or other."

"Well," said Grandma."I think it belonged to his family. There is a lady who often goes to look at the windows. We need to find her."

"That would be Lady Emily. She lives on The Rise," said Mr West.

"It's all falling into place," said Grandma.

"I know what to put on the stained glass window now, Grandma," said Mark.

"Thank you Mr West, you have been most helpful."

"Let's go back to the cathedral, Grandma, she might be there. Or there may be a clue in the windows about the family."

"Slow down, Mark, give an old lady time to catch up!"

"Don't you think it's exciting, Grandma?"

"Yes, Mark, it looks as though we have come a full circle."

Entering the cathedral, a gentleman came forward to help them. Mark excitedly explained why they were there. He listened intently and then led them to the three stained glass windows."If you look at the final window, you can see the Manor House and gardens, with horses and a carriage. Then, the second window, you see the same house with soldiers on horseback, with a family group in the corner. The third window is a celebration of the end of the war."

"Thank you so much," said Grandma."Would it be possible to meet Lady Emily?"

"I think it could be arranged. I could ask her when she next comes to visit. She loves to talk about her family. Can you give me your telephone number, so I can get in touch? My name is Jeffrey."

"Thank you Mr…"

"No, just Jeffrey."

"Oh, I'm sorry. I am Gladys and this is, Mark, my grandson. Thank you for your time."

"My pleasure. Did I overhear the young gentleman say he is going to learn how to make windows like these?"

"That is correct."

"That is amazing. I wish him luck. Not many people know how."

"It used to be done by the monks, but King Henry VIII stopped that!"

"That man ruined so much that was beautiful!" said Grandma.

"Indeed," said Jeffrey."I must start to close the cathedral now."

"What is the time?" asked Grandma."4.30 pm, it takes a good half an hour to close everything down."

"Does it really. Thank you, again. Here is my number, I have written it down for you. We hope to hear from you soon. Come now, Mark, time to go home."

"Coming, Grandma. It's a fascinating place this, so old and so quiet. Can we come again? Do you think Lady Emily will meet us?"

"We shall see. Let us find the car and go home."

. . . .

The next evening, John came to collect Mark to take him to the school, where he was to start learning about stained glass windows. He was nervous but John said,"to relax. He wouldn't be asked to do anything at first. Just to watch and learn. To use osmosis."

"What's that, to learn by watching? Is it possible?" asked Mark.

"Yes," said John."I did it, but you must watch very carefully. All children learn from their parents that way at first."

"I'll do my best."

"No one can do more than that, Mark. Here we are, follow me."

Mark swallowed hard and followed John into the building. He told him where to sit. Mark watched others arrive, all sorts of ages. They all settled down, some laying work on their table. A man entered the room and sat at the front desk. He had long hair tied at the back and was wearing rough clothes and heavy boots. He welcomed everyone and then, Mark, as a new member. He called himself Luke. Everyone then started work on their projects, even Luke."Feel free to walk around Mark. Try not to touch anything or get in the way, just watch."

"Thank you," said Mark. So that is what he did. He found it fascinating, and he began to understand how it was done. Time soon passed and then John took him home.

"Do you understand a bit more now, Mark?"

"Yes, I do. It's fascinating."

"You can work at your own pace. You have a window to design first. Luke will help you when you are ready. Bye for now, see you next week."

"How did you get on, Mark?"

"I'm learning by osmosis, Dad."

"Best way son, that's how I learnt to cook!"

"Really, Dad?" Mark went shopping for a sketch pad and pens and spent many hours looking at the Manor House, trying to design his window.

His dad knew about the house because, during the war, it was neat and tidy. There were gardeners working on the gardens."Did you ever see inside the house, Dad?" asked Mark.

"No son, it was private property back then and the war office was in charge of it. It was definitely out of bounds then. We used to see a lot of horses."

"Did the horses belong to the original family?"

"I don't think so, Mark. That was during the war."

"We are trying to meet Lady Emily. She is the last living member of the family."

"Is she? Well, she will be able to tell you all about the house history and the family."

"That is what we are hoping. Thanks for letting me go to the classes, Dad."

"Let's hope you enjoy learning, Mark."

"Thanks, Dad, for giving me the chance."

"Here is Grandma, maybe she has some news."

"She might have."

"Hello, Gran, any news?"

"Yes, Mark. I've had a phone call from Jeffrey at the cathedral. Lady Emily will be pleased to meet us at the cathedral on Wednesday afternoon."

"Oh, Gran, that's wonderful!"

"I shall come for you after lunch, then we can go and hear what she has to tell us."

"Thanks, Gran. Would you like some tea?"

"Yes, please, Mark. I'll just sit in the garden."

"Okay, I'll bring it out to you. Do you want one, Dad?"

"Yes, I will. Thank you son." So they sat, drank tea and chatted about stained glass windows and the houses being built in Windmill Crescent, until it began to get quite chilly. Then, Grandma got up to go.

"See you on Wednesday, Mark."

"Yes, I shall be ready."

. . . .

Wednesday dawned bright and dry and Mark woke early. He helped his mum by laying the breakfast table. He was excited about the afternoon and told his mum about it. She said it was a wonderful opportunity to learn about the history of the Manor House and she would be most interested to hear his news this evening when he got back. They chatted over breakfast and time soon went.

Mark did his chores as quickly as he could and helped his mother. He was almost too excited to eat his lunch, but his mother understood. It was time. Grandma arrived and they were soon on their way to meet Lady Emily."Have you got any questions ready, Mark?"

"Yes, I have, Grandma, but we must let her talk first."

"Of course, this will bring many memories back for her."

They parked the car and walked to the cathedral. There they found seated, in front of the three windows, an elderly lady."You go first, Gran." So, Grandma walked towards her, holding out her hand.

"Lady Emily, I am so pleased to meet you. This is my grandson, Mark."

"Hello," said Mark."This is so exciting. The windows are lovely, is that your home in the first one?"

"Yes, it is, Mark. As it used to look. I'm afraid the soldiers did a lot of damage when they occupied it, especially to the ballroom. The floor is a disgrace now."

"What a pity," said Grandma."Hob-nailed boots are no good for dancing, are they?"

"You are right. We had the most beautiful balls there with a full orchestra."

"Really, it was a different age then."

"Surely you remember it Mrs…"

"Please call me Gladys, Lady Emily. Yes, I remember, but of course I didn't live in such a grand house."

"The windows onto the garden were flung open, so if you walked in the garden you could still hear the music. One of my partners waltzed me right down the path to the bower, just to steal a kiss."

"How romantic, Lady Emily. Did you marry him?"

"No, he was killed in the war, so sad."

"Was Sir Jeremy your father?" asked Mark.

"No, he was my grandfather."

"Such beautiful windows."

"They are, they give me such comfort."

"You had horses and carriages then?" asked Mark.

"Oh yes, and I had my own horse to ride. We had more land then. All of Manor Road Estate was our land."

"That is where we live. I want to make a stained glass window for the house, showing your house," Mark finished in a rush.

"How lovely, you must show me it when it is done."

"It will take about six months from start to finish. I have to design it first."

"Would you like to come up to the house to see it close up?" asked Lady Emily.

"Yes, please!" Mark was overwhelmed by her generosity.

"We will arrange it through Jeffrey, here at the cathedral."

"Of course," said Grandma."Now we will leave you and thank you for your time, M'Lady."

"It has been a pleasure and I shall be most interested to see your design, Mark."

"Thank you, Lady Emily."

They left the cathedral, pleased to have talked to Lady Emily and looking forward to more in the future. In the car, Mark said,"She was so generous and helpful."

"Yes, she was, Mark. I think you have given her something to look forward to."

"That's great. I shall have to get going on my design."

That evening, he told his parents all about the meeting. His mother was thrilled."I would like to see inside the house."

"Did you ask how old it was?" asked Mother.

"No, I didn't. She talked about the balls and the music. She had her own horse, and this estate was part of their land."

"How difficult it must be for her to see houses, where she once rode her horse."

"It was her grandfather who had the windows made that are in the cathedral, and she wants to see my design and finished window."

"Goodness, does she?" said his mother.

"You had better get on with it then," said his father.

"Yes, I must, Dad. It's rather daunting though!"

"Why don't you go to the library and see if they have any pictures of the Manor House, or if there is a book that has been written about it?"

"Great, Dad, I never thought of that. We could go tomorrow."

"But that would leave Grandma out?"

"Ask her to come."

"Yes, I will. Thanks, Dad."

. . . .

The next day, Grandma arrived. She was so pleased to have been asked."Your clever father, thinking of the library. I wonder why I didn't?"

"Gran, you can't think of everything!"

"I know, but I should have thought of the library. Now where is he?"

"Gone to get the car, Grandma."

"Oh, we are honoured. Is he taking us?"

"Yes, here he is."

"Are we ready then. Mother, you sit in the front and, Mark can have the whole of the back seat."

"Where is your mother, Mark?"

"She has friends coming today."

"What a pity," said Grandma.

Off they went. Unbeknown to them all, Father had already rung the library and primed them what they were looking for. So, when they arrived Jane the Librarian, was ready and waiting.

"I've found some photographs," she said. Leading them to a desk at the rear of the library. There laid out were half a dozen photographs.

"Look, Dad, there is one of the Manor."

"Yes, I see. Thank you, Jane."

"There are three interior shots here. One of the ballroom, the library and the kitchen."

"Is that the cook?" asked Mark.

"I think it must have been."

"Do we know how old these photographs are? Would the cook still be alive?"

"I couldn't say," said Jane,"but we could look at the census records."

"What are they?" said Mark.

"Every ten years, starting in 1901, a record was made of every family."

"Everyone?"

"Yes, everyone. Let's look at 1901 and see who was living in the Manor House then. From the paper records the information has been transferred to computer."

"I have looked at some myself for our family," said Dad,"they are very helpful."

Jane set up the computer and they moved around it watching her scroll through the entries until she found the right one."Now let's see who was there. There is a Lord Charles and his wife Lady Veronica and three sons and a daughter, Josephine."

"No Emily?" asked Mark.

"Too soon," said Grandma,"she was not born yet."

"Isn't it difficult sorting out the years."

"If you remember, Emily said her grandfather Jeremy, had the windows made."

"Yes, and he is not shown here in 1901."

"Can we see the next one?" asked Mark.

"Of course," said Jane.

Grandma interrupted."Look, Mark at how many people worked at the Manor at that time. There is a cook, housekeeper, butler, four housemaids, two grooms, two gardeners, it was a busy place."

"Gosh, Grandma, it was!"

"Can we look at 911 now Jane?"

"Yes, I have it here." Jane changed the reel and found the details they wanted.

"Look, there is Lord Jeremy, and he is married to Charlotte. They have a son and daughter. I expect one of those is Emily's parents."

"Maybe she will be on the next reel, if she was home," said Mark.

"There are less servants now," said Grandma."Just two maids, one groom and the cook is a Mrs Wilson."

"Now," said Dad,"remember there was a war within the next ten years and things changed."

"Yes," said Grandma,"let's see the next one."

"This is 1921," said Jane."That would be three years from the end of the first World War. There was an influenza pandemic in 1918 that killed thousands of people."

"You have to know your history, doing this," said Mark.

"That's right, Mark," said Dad.

"Here we are," said Jane,"there were a lot less people counted in this year."

"Look, Lord Jeremy is still here, but he is old. His wife has gone, no son and only a daughter," said Jane.

"She is married now."

"Yes, so she is. Could she be Emily's mum?"

"It's possible," said Grandma.

"We didn't ask Emily about her parents, did we, Gran?"

"No, we didn't, Mark, but it's not too late and there are more reels to look at."

"The next is 1931," said Jane."No Lord Jeremy. In fact, no lord at all. His son must have died in the war. Edwina, his daughter and her husband Charles, have a baby daughter Emily. She's three years old."

"There she is," said Mark, with great satisfaction!

"There is only one groom, one gardener and a cook, Agatha Chine. The next reel will show the army in residence. As Emily didn't marry, or have children, she is the last. So, when she dies that is the end of the family line."

"How sad," said Grandma.

"Well, Mark," says Dad,"you are the last male in our family. If you don't have children, our family will finish."

"That's a big responsibility," said Mark.

"Thank you Jane," said Dad,"you have been a great help."

"I am pleased to be of help," replied Jane."There does not appear to have been any books written about the Manor."

Everyone got up to leave, thanking Jane.

Grandma said,"Perhaps an advert in the paper might draw out any people that worked at the Manor, that are still alive."

"That would be a long shot."

"Yes, it would. Still, we have gained an awful lot today!" They left the library and went to a local café for a drink and sandwich.

"I think," said Mark,"I will ask my tutor for help on my window design."

"Well done," said Grandma,"it is not easy, is it?"

"Grandma, where do we go from here?" said Mark.

"I'm not sure, Mark. Perhaps, you should concentrate on your window. Emily would like to see it and she is not getting any younger."

"That is true. I'll do that on Thursday."

Thursday came at last and when everyone had arrived and was settled, Mark approached the tutor, Luke."I'm wondering if you will help me with my design, please, Luke."

"Of course, I will, Mark. First, what thoughts have you had already?"

Mark took a deep breath."Well, my house, in fact the whole area of houses, was built on the land that belonged to the Manor House. So, I feel the Manor should be shown. I have spoken to Lady Emily who is the last surviving member of the family, and she has told me she used to ride her pony where the houses are now."

"That is a good start, Mark. So we have a Manor House, a lady riding countryside. What animals and trees did she notice?" said Luke.

"Can we go to the house to sketch?"

"Mark, I'm sure we can. Should I arrange it? What day is best for you? I think we should ask the lady first, Mark."

"Alright, I will do that," said Mark.

"In the meantime, sketch the scene roughly to give us some idea."

"Thank you, Luke."

"Don't worry, Mark, we will make it work and I think it will be good."

"Thank you."

"Go and start your sketch then."

So, Mark returned to his desk and started to draw. By the time John called for them to go, he had a reasonable sketch to show him."What do you think, John, it's only a rough idea as yet?"

"We all start with rough ideas, Mark, but it looks good," said John.

"Thanks, John, we should go home now."

When he got home, his dad was there to greet him."How did you get on, Mark?"

"Great, Dad. I've got a rough sketch. Here it is. Here's the Manor House and drive with trees behind and here is Lady Emily riding her pony on what is now, Manor Road."

"I see. What else is to go in?"

"Possibly some animals, birds and more trees. It will depend on what Lady Emily has to say," said Mark.

"Well, you have made a good start."

"Is Mum still up?"

"No, Mark."

"I'll show her in the morning."

"Goodnight, Dad."

"Goodnight, Mark."

. . . .

The next day, Mark showed his sketch to his mum. She studied it carefully and listened to his explanation and then hugged him. She asked,"Is this to go over our front door?"

"Yes," said Mark,"it will take about six months to make."

"How wonderful, and to have it made by my own son. Will you be making one for Gran too?"

"Probably, Mum. Isn't it exciting and I owe Grandma for getting me interested in the first place. I'm going to see if they have started to build her house yet."

"Yes, they have. She was telling me yesterday. Everything is changing, Mark."

"For the better I hope, Mum. Do you want to come with me?"

"Not this morning, Mark. Your dad and I are going out. Another time."

"Okay, Mum, bye for now." As Mark walked onto the estate, he saw a 'sold' Board on Windmill House. He was pleased about this. Soon there would be more people about and the place would come alive. Mark walked further on, seeing how the next phase was coming along. There he found Grandma, waving at him. He quickened his steps, calling out to her,"I'm glad you are here. Did you see that Windmill House is sold?"

"Yes, I did, Mark. I'm very pleased for Robert…his first sale."

"No, Gran, his second, you bought one."

"So I did. Come see, Mark."

They walked together to Grandma's plot and Mark could see the footings waiting for the concrete."It won't take long once the concrete is in, will it, Gran?"

"You're right, Mark. The trucks are due today. That is why I came."

"I'm glad I came on the right day," said Mark."It doesn't look very big when you see it like this, does it?"

"No, Mark, it doesn't, but it will be big enough for me as long as there is a garden."

"Look I can see a truck coming."

"Oh good." They watched together as the concrete was poured.

"Do you remember doing this at Windmill House, Mark?"

"Yes, I do, Gran, and then it was built very quickly. Do you still want a stained glass window?"

"Yes, please, Mark."

"Have you thought what you want on it?"

"Yes, I have. It must have the windmill, but not as large as the one in Windmill House and then all the natural flowers and I want a robin."

"Well thanks, Gran, I shall look forward to doing that. What do you mean by natural flowers?"

"I mean those that grow naturally here. Like the primroses, bluebells, dandelions and rag robbin."

"I'll have to get a flower book."

"I'll get you one for Christmas, Mark."

"Thank you. I'll have to do Mum and Dad's first, but now I can plan ahead."

"Here is the next truck. Nearly done." Mark left his excited Gran and walked home deep in thought.

"I must contact Lady Emily and arrange a visit to the Manor. I'll do that when I get home. Life is so busy but so interesting. I shall look forward to meeting the new owners of Windmill House. I wonder what Gran will call her house?"

When he got home, the house was empty. He sat by the telephone and found Jeffrey's number and dialled it. Jeffrey was there and Mark explained about his need for himself and his tutor to visit the Manor if Lady Emily could spare the time. Jeffrey said he would try and arrange it."When do you want to go?" he asked Mark.

"Whenever it suits Lady Emily. I have a preliminary sketch, but we need to get her details right."

"I understand. Give me your telephone number, Mark, and I'll call you back." Mark gave over the number and rang off.

He looked at the sketch again and tried to visualise it finished. Then gave up and raided the fridge for his lunch which Mum had left for him. She had asked him what he wanted for his birthday and thought to ask for a Rescue dog. He could take the dog everywhere with him as a companion. A quiet one, nothing boisterous and likely to pull him over. But then, maybe his parents wouldn't want a dog in the house? He would ask them when they returned home.

"We don't mind a dog, Mark, but not a puppy."

"I don't want a puppy. An older one that I can take everywhere with me. Can I come and choose?"

"Of course you can, we'll make arrangements." I shall need a diary soon for all of these appointments, thought Mark. The telephone rang. His dad went to answer it.

"It's for you, Mark, it's Jeffrey."

"Thanks, Dad. Hello Jeffrey, you were quick getting back!"

"Lady Emily will be pleased to meet you at the Manor House this Thursday at 11.00am. Will that be alright?"

"Yes, I think so. I'll check with my tutor and ring you back. Thank you."

"My pleasure, Mark, bye for now."

Mark was beaming when he came off the phone."Good news, Mark?" asked his mum.

"Yes, very. I must ring my tutor; can I use the telephone, please, Mum?"

"Yes, of course you can, Mark." After a couple of tries, he got through to Luke.

"Luke, Lady Emily has suggested this Thursday at 11.00am to visit. Is that alright with you?"

"Yes, that will be fine. Are we picking her up? Look, I'll leave you to make the arrangements, Mark, OK?"

"Alright, I'll get back to you. I'm sorry, Mum, Dad, this is taking longer than I thought it would. I need to ring Jeffrey again."

"That's alright. What are you trying to arrange?"

"A visit to the Manor House with my tutor to help finalise the picture."

"Well, go ahead," said Dad.

Having dialled Jeffrey again and agreed the time and day would be agreeable. He sank into the armchair to think. Then remembered Gran. Where was she? In the garden…where else!"Grandma, would you like some tea?"

"Yes, please, Mark. Any news?"

"Yes, I'll tell you when I bring the tea." It didn't take long to boil the kettle, make the tea and a juice for himself. He found some biscuits and put them on a plate, then everything was put on a tray and he set off to the garden.

"This is nice, Mark. Do you want a chair?"

"No, thanks, Gran, I'll sit on the grass."

"Now, what's the latest, Mark?"

"On Thursday at 11.00am we are to meet Lady Emily at the Manor House. Would you like to come?"

"Of course, I wouldn't want to miss it. I hope we can see inside."

"We will have to see how much time we have and whether she wants us to go inside, Gran."

"Of course. By the way, I have put an advert in the paper for any staff that worked at the house in days gone by."

"Have you, Gran, I wonder if anyone will reply?"

"We shall have to wait and see. Something to look forward to."

"Gran, have you decided on a name for your new house yet?"

"Yes, I shall call it Windmill Cottage," replied Gran.

"That sounds just right."

"Being early has its advantages."

"I wonder what will others call theirs?"

"That's another thing to look forward to. They might just accept a house number."

"Isn't there just two more to be built, Gran?"

"Yes, that's right, Mark."

"You will soon have neighbours and life will be busy for you with your garden."

"Your dad has offered to dig and help me plant it."

"Good for Dad!"

"Sorry, Gran, but I have to make another phone call to Jeffrey if I am not too late."

"You must hurry. It's gone four o'clock."

"Is it, gosh, I'd better hurry."

"Don't worry about the tray, Mark, I'll see to it."

"Thanks, Gran."

Mark sped into the house and dialled Jeffrey's number."Hello Jeffrey, I should have told you that we will pick up Lady Emily at 11.00am on Thursday if that will be alright."

"Does she live on the Rise?"

"Yes, number ten."

"Thanks." Well, that's done and arranged. I had better confirm this with Luke and tell him that Grandma is coming as well.

Picking up the phone he dialled Luke's number."Hello, Luke, it's Mark. It's okay to pick up Lady Emily at eleven o'clock and my grandma would like to come too. She has already met Lady Emily. Is that okay?"

"That's fine, Mark. The two ladies can chat. I'll collect you and your grandma at 9.45 on Thursday. It will soon come!"

"Oh, and, Luke, my grandma is buying a bungalow in Windmill Crescent and wants a stained-glass window."

"Does she now. We seem to be starting a trend, Mark. That is good. Bye for now."

"Bye, Luke. Nobody mentions money. They must cost something. Gran will want to know; I'll have to ask my tutor. My teacher used to say...If you don't ask, you don't get. I will ask."

....

Thursday came and it was a rainy day."Oh, no!"

"Don't worry son, the forecast says it will brighten up by midday."

"I hope you're right, Dad. How can we sketch in the rain?"

"Under a brolly of course."

"Of course," said Mark,"why didn't I think of that?" After breakfast, it did look brighter and had stopped raining. By the time Luke arrived and, Grandma, it was much better. Mum had prepared a packed lunch.

Grandma said,"I think we may see inside the house, especially if we have more rain."

"You may be right," said Luke."Now, are we all ready?"

"I think so."

"Well, you are not, Mark, you still have your slippers on!" said Mum.

"It's alright, Mum, my boots are in the porch."

"Good, don't forget now."

"No, I won't."

"Luke, will you take the lunch? Mind it's heavy."

"It sure is, how many for lunch. Is the army coming?" joked Luke.

"No, Luke, they left years ago," said Mark, laughing.

So, off they went to the car and Mum said quietly to Dad,"I wish I was going."

"I'm sure you will hear all about it when they return."

"Yes, I know, but it's not the same as being there."

"Oh, I forgot the brolly."

"I didn't, it's in the car."

"Thank you, what would I do without you?" said Grandma.

"Oh, you will manage, and you will have, Mark." Turning and waving, they entered the house.

When they all arrived at the Manor House, it had stopped raining."Thank goodness for that," said Grandma. Lady Emily agreed."But dare we leave the umbrellas in the car?" said Grandma, peering at the clouds.

"Let's chance it. If needed, Mark can get them, he's the fastest," said Luke. Mark and Luke were already getting their sketch books ready.

"Here," said Luke,"this looks like a good spot. Lady Emily, is all we can see from here the original house?"

"Yes, except for that window," she pointed."The wall was there, but not the window."

"Who would have put that window in?" asked Mark.

"I really don't know. It wasn't there when we lived here," replied Lady Emily.

"Another mystery," said Mark.

"Never mind," said Luke,"we will draw it without the window."

"What about the trees?"

"Yes, except that silver birch. It must have seeded itself."

"Life goes on," muttered Luke, beginning to sketch.

Mark watched, fascinated as the picture took shape on the page."Shall we take it from another angle?" said Luke.

"Looks like we have a visitor," said Mark, watching a man on a bicycle coming up the drive.

"Are you expecting anyone?"

Lady Emily said,"No."

"Oh, but I was," said Gran.

"Gran, what are you up to now?"

"Just a little surprise."

Suddenly, Lady Emily gasped."Is that you, Jake? Oh, how lovely. Do you know where my pony is now? This is Jake everyone. He used to look after my pony."

Jake took of his cap, touched his forehead and grinned.

"Yes, M'Lady, how lovely to see you. Your pony is being used to teach children to ride, at a local riding school. I go there to help and look after her. She is getting old now."

"She's still alive!" exclaimed Lady Emily."How wonderful. Will you take me to see her?"

"I certainly will."

"Grandma, what happened?"

"Well, Mark, Jake answered my advert and I asked him to come today."

"That's brilliant!"

"Can we get on before it rains again?" said Luke.

"Yes, of course. Jake and I will catch up on the news later but thank you for finding him. Here was I thinking I was the only one left. Go and look at the stable, Jake," said Lady Emily.

"Yes, M'Lady," and off he went.

"Shall we go over there?" said Luke,"get a different angle."

"Yes, I'll lead the way," said Lady Emily, then she moved on.

"Yes, that's good," said Luke, turning to a blank page.

"How many bedrooms are there?"

"There were forty-five, but I don't know what happened during the army stay. Look, why don't we go inside, then you will get a better idea. I warn you; it will be dirty."

"But not wet," said Grandma, as she watched a shower coming in.

They made their way to the big main doors and Lady Emily produced a big key to unlock them."Still the same key?" asked Luke.

"Yes, that did not change." In they went into the great hall, with a sweeping staircase ahead, in front of them.

"This is wonderful," said Grandma, moving closer to Lady Emily."You must have so many memories?"

"I have. I still get quite emotional," Lady Emily replied.

Luke was sketching."Were there pictures here?" he asked.

"Lots, and all the way up the stairs. They are in storage now."

"Perhaps, one day, you can have an exhibition," said Mark, excitedly.

"I don't know, Mark. Perhaps, after I am gone."

"Now, don't talk like that Lady Emily," said Grandma,"you must enjoy your latter years, like me. I'm about to move house and Mark is going to make me a stained-glass window. You must come and have tea with me when I am settled."

"Yes, please, I haven't gone out for tea for a long while."

"That's settled then," said Grandma,"life can still be exciting at our age. Mark and I have some good days out, don't we, Mark?"

"We sure do, Grandma."

"We are doing the family tree at the moment, which is very interesting."

"Perhaps, I should do mine," sighed Lady Emily.

"Why not," said Grandma,"we will help, won't we, Mark?"

"Of course, we will."

"But, Mark has so many windows to make and we have forgotten Luke."

"Don't worry about me," said Luke,"as long as I have something to sketch."

"Would you do the fireplace in this room, for me please?" leading the way.

"What a stunner, you could roast an ox in there, and they probably did!" said Luke.

"Yes, it was known that you couldn't get into this room for the heat."

Luke sat on his haunches and began to sketch."Where can we have our picnic, Lady Emily?"

"In the kitchen. I think that would be the best place," answered Lady Emily, leading the way to the kitchen.

"We'll leave some for you, Luke," Mark called out.

"Thanks, Mark. I won't be long."

"What a big kitchen," gasped Grandma,"and another large fireplace." Grandma produced a cloth and covered the table. She began to lay out the plates, cutlery and food.

"Your mum has done us proud, Mark."

"Yes, she has," eyeing the feast, with a growing boy's hunger, just waiting to be let loose."

"Here I am," said Luke,"just in time I see."

"I'm sorry there are no chairs," said Lady Emily.

"Never mind, we will eat off the hoof," said Luke, whilst helping himself to a sandwich.

"These are nice. Do have one Lady Emily."

"Thank you," she replied,"I am really enjoying our visit, you have made it fun."

"And, so it should be. Eat up everyone. Here, Mark, take this plateful to Jake in the stables," said Grandma.

"Oh dear, I had forgotten about Jake, but then, he wouldn't have come into the house. Thank you, Grandma, for remembering."

Mark picked up the plate and set off for the stables. What a great day, he thought. Jake was very pleased not to have been forgotten."You know, Mark, it's all a bit sad. This stable used to house twenty horses, all stomping and chomping about. It was warm and lovely."

"I find it difficult to imagine," replied Mark,"I expect it's all so different now."

"How it's changed over the years, I do miss it. Still, I work with the horses at the riding stable to keep my hand in. Do you ride, Mark?"

"No, Jake, I don't. I don't know where I would find the time, or the money."

"Yes, it can be expensive," said Jake.

"Will you come into the house, Jake?"

"No, not me, it's not my place."

"Times have changed," said Mark.

"Not for me they ain't. Thank you for the food. I'm quite happy here but would like some straw."

"Only Gran knew you were coming, Jake."

"Yes, she's a lovely lady, Mark."

"I know. She is my grandma; she makes my life so interesting."

"You are lucky. I never remember my grandparents. We don't appreciate them when we have them. Only after they are gone do we think of all the questions we could have asked. Too late then!"

"Here's your plate Mark and thank you. Perhaps, I'll see you again at the riding school. You don't have to ride, just visit. M'Lady will come and visit her pony. She won't have forgotten her."

"Bye," said Mark, taking the plate from Jake.

When he got back to the kitchen, nearly all the food had gone, but there was a drink waiting for him."I'd better take a drink to Jake."

"I'll do it," said Luke, picking up the cup and setting off.

"What a wonderful picnic," said Lady Emily."I'm quite full. I used to come here quite often. It was always so warm and busy with beautiful smells and always a piece of cake to be had! The young are always hungry," she said, smiling down at Mark, who grinned back, agreeing.

Luke returned."Interesting chap. We had a good conversation."

"Lovely. Now, Luke, do you have enough sketches?" asked Lady Emily.

"I do, thank you, and I now have the feel of the place. Was there a library!"

"There was, but all of the books have gone now, mostly sold of course. It's starting to get dark, and we have had a long and fruitful day."

"Yes, we have," said Mark."Thank you for allowing us into the house. Could we see the ballroom, I've never seen one."

"Yes, of course you can but I warn you the floor is ruined. Follow me." Which they did.

"They certainly did ruin it," said Grandma.

"I should put it right and send the bill to the government, what a disgrace."

"I don't have the money to put it right and I don't think they would pay for it. It was all up to my father then."

"Of course it was." said Grandma.

"Luke, could you carry the picnic remains for me, please."

"Yes, of course. Let's get in the car before it rains again."

"What about Jake. Would his bike fit in?" asked Mark.

"Don't worry about me, I'll ride home it's not too far. Thank you M'Lady for allowing me to visit." said Jake.

"I will visit my pony so we shall meet again, Jake. What a day!"

Into the car they clambered, laughing and very pleased with themselves."Thank you," said Lady Emily,"I feel as though I have made new friends."

"So you have, and you must stop hiding away," said Grandma. And so, the day ended happily, and Grandma and Mark sat around the tea table telling his mum and dad all about it.

Then, Grandma said,"I have invited Lady Emily for tea in my new house and you must all come as well."

"How lovely said his mum and especially that the pony has been found as well."

His dad smiled and then said,"Gladys, while you were out there was a phone call for you. I think it's someone about your advert in the paper. The details are by the phone."

"Thank you, Son."

Grandma went over to the telephone and picked up the notepad. She called for Mark."It's the daughter of the cook. Her mother's not well but would love to meet and talk next Tuesday at the care home, at 10.30 am."

"That's brilliant," said Mark."I wonder if Lady Emily would want to come."

"We shall have to ask her," said Gran.

"I will ring Jeffrey."

"Everything keeps happening," said Mark's mum.

"Yes," said Gran,"we didn't know what would happen when we started this adventure. See what can happen when you are interested and ask questions, Mark."

"Yes, Gran. You have an adventure and I still haven't made the window yet!"

"Let's clear away now, it's getting late."

"Thank you, for the splendid picnic, there's not much left," said Mark.

"There was enough then?"

"Plenty, Gran, even Jake got fed." And so that day ended.

. . . .

"Today," said Mark,"I shall see Luke and hopefully make a start on the window."

"John arrived to collect him and had already heard about their day, from Luke. He had shown him the sketches."

"All looks good, Mark."

"Yes, it does, but we haven't seen the pony yet."

"But she has been found." They went in and made ready. As soon as Luke sat down, Mark went to him.

"Have we got enough, Luke?"

"For the moment we have. We shall have to visit the pony if she is to be included."

"I think so. The connection has to be made between the Manor House land and the Manor House road," said Mark.

"Exactly!" agreed Luke."So we will have to arrange a visit as I have a picture to perfect."

"What picture?" asked Mark.

"Do you remember, Mark. Lady Emily asked me to sketch the fireplace for her?"

"Yes, I do."

"Well, it appears she wants to frame it as a memory. So, we had a chat and now know how to prepare it for framing."

"Can I see it when it's done, please?"

"Of course, Mark, I will show it to you. Let's break to your window. Here are your sketches, which view do you want?"

"The first I think, Luke."

"I'm inclined to agree with you, Mark. That one includes a tree, which looks better."

"Now, before you do any more to your project I want you to join Graeme over there. He is about to begin to put his picture together. Watch and learn and help if you can." So, Mark found himself with Graeme wondering what would happen next.

First he showed Mark his sketch, which he had coloured in with numbers in each colour."I haven't done that yet, Graeme," said Mark.

"You will find it helps at the next stage." Mark studied the picture carefully.

"What are these numbers?"

"Each coloured glass has a number. So the number tells me which colour glass to use and where," replied Graeme.

"I see," said Mark.

"But first we must go slowly and carefully so we don't make a mistake. Can you fetch me the tracing paper, please, Mark?"

"Yes, sure. From this cupboard?"

"Yes, that's correct." Mark fetched the tracing paper wondering why, but as he watched he understood. Graeme was making templates, just like he had seen Grandma make when she was doing her patchwork.

"This would interest her," thought Mark. Slowly Graeme began to draw around the shapes with the numbers on. He then cut them out and transferred the number to the template. Soon he had a pile, but didn't stop until all were done, by which time it was lunch break.

We settled down to eat our sandwiches and Tom brought cups of tea, which was welcome. The one thing needed with this work was concentration and of course patience."I'm pleased with this morning's progress," said Graeme. At that point, Luke came over to see how he was progressing.

"You have made good progress, Graeme. Can I do some checking?"

"Of course," said Graeme,"it has to be right."

Luke took the top few templates and placed them on the picture."These two are good but this one I would do again. It looks a bit wavy. Check them all will you, before you cut the glass?"

"Yes, I will," replied Graeme, flushing.

"Don't worry, Graeme, sometimes we get a bit over anxious without realising it. Better to check."

"Will you help me, Mark?" asked Graeme.

"Yes," said Mark,"I'll be glad of something to do." And that's what they did. They found another that needed to be done again as well as the first one, Luke had found.

"Good. Now we know they are all right," said Graeme, smiling with relief.

"Will you give me a hand when I do mine?" asked Mark.

"Yes, if I can. Luke might send someone else to you, like he did with us. Anyway, now I shall need you to find and fetch for me."

"Jolly good," said Mark, ready to help.

"First, I must decide which way to work. Top down or bottom up." He finally decided bottom up and they sorted through the templates for the first shapes.

"First," said Graeme,"find me the lead tape. There should be a roll on the bottom shelf." Mark knew what it looked like and soon located it."Thanks, Mark. Now the two small sections come first. Sometimes, a sheet of glass can get broken or nearly used and the bits are then put in separate bags that are numbered. See if these two numbers are available on the fragment list, which is on the right hand side of the door." Mark looked and found one of the numbers, but not the other."Find the bag for that number and then look for a complete sheet for the other number. Be very careful!" warned Graeme.

Mark did as asked and watched Graeme empty the fragments onto a tray, placing the template on the pieces."That piece will do," he said, as he placed it on his template. Then returning the other fragments back to their bag, Mark returned the bag to the cupboard."Can you fetch me a glass cutter please, Mark? There in that blue box on the second shelf." Mark did and watched Graeme as he fixed his template to the fragment and, using his tray, began to trace around it with the glass cutter.

Finally, he was satisfied and with crossed fingers, prepared to snap the glass. Three sides were quick, but the fourth needed more cutting. He then dropped it into place in his window. The first piece. He then took up the lead. At this point Luke appeared."Well done, the first piece. It is always exciting to see a picture build. I've come to help with the lead. You must not burn yourself." He carefully measured around the glass piece and marked the lead."We now need to go to the back section to do this."

So off they went, following Luke. There was a small bunsen burner alight and Luke stretched the lead mark over it, making it soften. On the bench was a sharp knife with which he cut the lead at the mark. Putting the roll under the bench out of the way, he proceeded to soften the piece."This, Graeme, should be soft enough, fetch your plate." Which Graeme did and Luke placed the hot lead on it.

"Now, back to your picture. Can you remember how to do it?"

"Yes, I think so, but please stay."

"I will," said Luke.

Mark watched as Graeme found a pair of pliers and picked up the lead. He placed it on the edge of the glass and taking another tool, began to shape the lead. When he had it around the glass, he began to press it down firmly to hold the glass in place."That's good," said Luke,"your first piece. You see how it's done now, Mark?"

"Yes, yes I do. I haven't coloured or numbered mine yet."

"That will be your next job, when you are ready to come back to me."

"Yes, I will, but I will stay and help Graeme some more."

"Good lad." Luke made his way to his desk where another student stood and waited with his sketch. Graeme, who was very pleased, picked up his second template and reached for a sheet of glass. He checked the number before putting it in place, near an edge, then began to cut. Mark placed a finger on the template to keep it still.

"Thanks, Mark," said Graeme, who began to snap the glass and the second piece dropped into place. Both were green of different shades. They went back to the bench for the lead and Graeme carefully measured and marked the lead and then back to heat it. He took his plate and pliers with him this time and pressed the lead into place.

"What number glass do you need now, Graeme?" Graeme gave Mark the template with the number on and said it would have to be a sheet. Mark soon found it and decided to stay with him until the end of the time. He was as delighted as Graeme, to see four pieces in his picture."I can't wait to start mine!" cried Mark. Then it was time to leave with John. He no doubt bored him with his chatter on the way home, but he didn't show it. Mark was full of his evening experience and couldn't wait to tell all about it.

Mark said goodnight to John and flew into the house where his parents were waiting. They knew what he was like. Gran was there as well. She was holding her sketch, her window design, so there was lots to talk about, until it was finally time for bed.

. . . .

The following day, when Mark awoke, the first thing he saw was Grandma's sketch. It was lovely, but looked a bit complicated, especially the flowers. He knew Luke would help him, he was sure, and with that thought, jumped out of bed."I will go to see Grandma's house. It must be nearly finished," he thought. After breakfast, he set off on his bike to the new housing estate. The 'for sale' board on Windmill House had a 'Sold' sticker on it. He noticed as he rode past. More bungalows were being built. Soon it will be alive with people and Grandma was talking to Robert outside her property. They looked nearly finished. They both called 'Good Morning' as Mark got off his bike, laying it down carefully on the path.

"Hello, Gran, hello, Robert. Is it nearly finished?" he asked.

"My work is almost done," said Robert,"just a bit of plastering to do in the bedrooms."

"Then I shall start on the garden," said Grandma.

"Oh, I have looked forward to this."

"I'll be away then," said Robert, striding across the road to one of the bungalows being built.

"Isn't it wonderful," said Grandma,"dreams coming true."

"Yes, I was looking at your sketch this morning. I'm well on my way with Mum and Dad's."

"Well done, Mark. Isn't life wonderful when there's so much to look forward to. Never did I think old age could offer me so much."

There she stood laughing at Mark and not looking her age at all. Mark thought, all because they'd asked questions and gone looking for the answers. I'll never be bored again. There's Dad delving back into the years, discovering the family and thoroughly enjoying himself. And then, Mum, trying to keep up with us all.

I said goodbye to Gran and cycled home again. Lunch was ready and Mark and his mum sat down together."Mum, do you feel left out that we have all discovered an interest, but not you?" asked Mark.

"Oh yes, I have. I'm interested in furniture and furnishings, and Gran and I are starting to explore this side of things, like colours and fabrics. That will keep us busy and give us hours of enjoyment."

"Marvellous. I was worried you were being left out."

"I was just waiting my time," said Mum.

"I shall help Gran with her garden."

"Of course, lovely, everyone's busy and happy. Your dad's thinking of writing a book."

"Is he, wow!"

The rest of the week seemed to pass quickly, and it was time to go with John to the class again. Luke gave Mark a box of coloured pencils, a sharpener and a sheet of colours with numbers against them to transfer to his sketch. Just as Graeme's had been. Soon I was busy colouring and numbering. When I was finished, I went over to Graeme to see how far he'd got and to see if I could help.

"Hullo, Mark, finished colouring?"

"Yes, do you need any help?"

"I need this numbered sheet of glass, if you could find it, please."

"I'll have a look. Your picture looks good, Graeme."

"It does. I am really pleased with it."

Mark went to the cupboard and soon brought back the numbered package. Graeme extracted the sheet from the pack.

"What a lovely blue," said Mark,"what is it for?"

"The lake see," said Graeme, pointing.

"That will really stand out," said Mark.

"I wanted a bright feature."

"I don't think I've got a bright feature," said Mark.

"Yes, you have," said Graeme."It may not be bright, but it is the castle."

"Hmm," said Mark, thinking it through and watching Graeme working."I'll get back to Luke if that's alright, Graeme?"

"Don't let me hold you back. You will want to get started."

Mark thought,"Yes, he did," as he made his way back to Luke with his finished sketch and pencils, paper and sharpener, which he was returning.

"Luke."

"Yes, what is it, Mark?"

"That tree in my sketch is a silver birch. How can I show bark in glass?"

"Well, initially, Mark, give it a brown trunk and later on by using white paint, you can put the bark markings on."

69

"I never thought of that."

"It's the same with the castle stone. Did you notice how it had been done in the cathedral pictures?"

"No, I didn't. I shall have to go back."

"Mark you have an hour, do you want to begin with a fragment for your first piece, or watch the others?"

"I think I will watch, Luke. Can I bring my grandmother's sketch next week? I think it needs to be simplified."

"Yes, bring it in. I'll take a look at it to see what can be done."

"Is your father still busy with the family tree?"

"Oh yes, very much so. He's thinking of writing a book."

"How interesting. I must come over and see how it is done. My niece has asked my help to do our family. Perhaps she should come as well," said Luke.

"Just give him a ring, he will be pleased to show you. He loves talking about it. I can't keep up with it. I think I shall wait for the book!"

Mark wandered around and watched all at various stages of the work. Graeme was out ahead with himself not far behind. John was doing his second one for Jeffrey, at the cathedral, but for his house. It looked very intriguing. Luke appeared by his side and said,"Jeffrey had wondered about giving a public showing. But perhaps thought the panels displayed, would speak for themselves. He was so pleased we were all busy. Robert had told him lots of people were looking and asking questions about the first one in Windmill House and soon there will be a second one on the estate, which again, will speak for itself. I am so pleased it's proving to be a success."

"I said it would," said John.

"You did, John, and you were right. We will carry on," said Luke. Mark went back to see Graeme.

"Where is your window going?" asked Mark.

"Mine is a present for my great aunt. She is ninety-five now and lives near the cathedral. She has always admired the windows saying, 'but they are only for the rich.' So, I decided to make her one."

"That is a brilliant idea, Graeme. So she doesn't know anything about it?"

"I hope not, Mark, if Jeffrey has kept my secret. I shall invite him to the unveiling."

"Can I come too?" asked Mark.

"Sure, you can, if I can come to yours. Your design is for your gran, isn't it?"

"Yes, but she knows about it and it is her sketch. I'll get it and show you." Mark left to get his sketch.

"That looks great, Mark," said Graeme."Those flowers could be tricky though."

"I've spoken to Luke about them to see if they can be simplified."

"Is he going to help?"

"Of course, doesn't he always," said Mark.

"Now don't take him for granted. Learn to do as much as you can for yourself. He won't always be here you know."

"He's not old, is he?" asked Mark.

"Older than you think," replied Graeme.

That gave Mark pause for thought. He decided he should try harder with drawing which he was aware was his weak point. Perhaps he should take some lessons. I suppose it is inevitable that we assume all older people will be there but realise they won't. We think we have all the time in the world, but sometimes there is a shock just around the corner. Mark thought he must get Gran's window finished, but first my parents."You have just given me a kick up the pants, Graeme, thanks."

"My pleasure, Mark," said Graeme, looking puzzled.

The next day, Mark made his way to the cathedral to look more closely at the stone work of the castle and trees. Jeffrey wasn't there and it was quiet. He was able to observe quietly another glass maker's artwork from long ago. He began to see the subtle additions in paint and understand the difference they made. He realised that he must observe more closely in future, it will make all the difference to his design.

He was just leaving when he saw the lady from the civic centre. She asked him how he was progressing. He enjoyed telling her all about it. She asked if she could see the design. He said she could, and he would let her know when it was finished. He then left to be home for tea. His mum was very quiet but appeared to be very pleased. Dad told Mark of Luke's phone call and said Luke was visiting tomorrow. Dad was quite pleased about this. Tea passed amicably in this way. Mark noticed swatches of material on the sideboard. Mum had begun. How the family was changing. Each with their own project. Mark spent the evening with his paints and paper, trying to get special effects like he had seen that afternoon. He tried to find art classes for himself without success. Perhaps, Luke could recommend someone.

Soon it was back to the class and his window. Starting with the fragments, he began. Graeme came over to assist him with his first lead piece which was a great help. Slowly, he gained confidence and took great pleasure as each piece was added. Slow but sure. There was no rush. Mark helped

Graeme in the afternoon. His was nearly finished. Won't his great aunt be surprised! Finally the last piece went in and Graeme breathed deeply.

He turned towards Mark and hugged him. Luke was watching and came over to congratulate him. John asked Graeme when he wanted him to fit it. Graeme couldn't think at that moment. It had taken so long to complete; he couldn't quite believe he had achieved it. There were tears in his eyes and Luke told him to sit down and gather his thoughts.

"John," he said,"I've somehow got to get my great aunt out of the house whilst the window was being fitted and I don't know how."

"Has she got any family she could visit for tea?" John asked.

"Yes, that's it, I shall arrange something."

"When is her birthday?" asked Mark.

"Birthday, birthday. March I think, not too far away."

"See what you can do secretly."

"Yes, yes," still bemused, he couldn't think straight.

"Graeme, just sit and look at your picture for the moment. It will all come clear, just relax," said Luke.

"It's been a long time since I had the idea. Thank you, Luke for helping me and you too, Mark."

"Our pleasure," said Luke and Mark together.

"Will I feel like this?" thought Mark."I don't think so, mine is not a surprise."

Soon everything calmed down and Graeme just sat and stared at his finished window. Everyone went back to their own work. Eventually, Luke wrapped his window and locked it in the glass cupboard. Everyone cleared up and left. The next day, Luke was on the phone to Mark."We have had a break in, Graeme's window has gone!"

"Was there anything else taken?" asked Mark.

"No, they've made a bit of a mess, but his was the only one taken and it was completed. The police are here and also Graeme, who is very upset. The police seem to think they will get it back. But we shall have to wait and see."

"Poor, Graeme, what a shock."

"We are obviously getting too well known, but amateurs won't know how or where to dispose of such a window. It won't suit everyone. It's nice to have the publicity but definitely not this sort," said Luke.

"Is my…"

"Yes, Mark, yours is safe and sound."

"Thank goodness."

They all set to work cleaning up. The telephone rang.

"Hello," said Luke."Yes, inspector, any news?"

"Yes, we have had two gentlemen on the phone reporting being offered a stained glass window for £500. We are getting a description of both the person and the van in question. It won't be long before we have them."

"Thank you, inspector," said Luke."Well, the inspector says two people have come forward with information."

"That's great," said Graeme, who now had nothing to do.

"Graeme, could you give Mark a hand?"

"Yes, of course, good to have something to do. Hello, Mark, can I help?"

"Yes, please, Graeme. Could you check my colours and numbers are correct, like I did for you?"

"Yes," said Graeme,"it's good to have a second check."
The phone rang again.

"Hello, inspector, Luke here."

"We have located the van but haven't moved in yet."

"Good. Remember, inspector, the contents are fragile."

"We won't forget," replied the inspector.

"The police have located the van," said Luke.

"Wonderful, I shall get my window back!" cried Graeme, grinning from ear to ear.

"Calm down. It hasn't been recovered yet."

"Sorry, Luke, I'll help Mark while I'm waiting." Slowly, Mark's window began to take shape to his great delight. They did the trunk of the tree and Mark explained to Graeme it was a silver birch so he would need white paint on the trunk to give the right effect."That's new to me," said Graeme,"I shall watch carefully."

Mark stopped and thought. He didn't know if he could achieve the effect he wanted. He approached Luke about art lessons and said he'd like some. Did Luke know an art teacher.

"Yes, Mark, I will teach you for a fee."

"Of course," said Mark.

"I am seeing your dad tomorrow and I will discuss it with him then. Is that alright?" asked Luke.

"Yes, of course. He will be paying after all."

"Luke, what about the pony?"

"Look carefully at your window, Mark. Where would you put it and what do you want the focal point to be?"

"The Manor House," replied Mark.

"Exactly."

"So we leave the pony out?" asked Mark.

"Yes, if you agree." Mark produced the sketch and had to agree with Luke's suggestion.

"It would look a bit crowded; I think."

"Right, then carry on as you were."

"Thank you, Luke."

"I'm just so pleased we have so much work and we are beginning to be noticed. Not much money yet, but it will come," said Luke.

Mark went back to find Graeme and found him making templates."Gosh, thanks," said Mark, ready to take over again. Graeme pointed out where he had got to and Mark carried on. Soon it was done, and Luke came to check it over.

"Just one should be done again and then you can start, Mark."

"Just one, thanks, Graeme."

"How are you working, top or bottom first?" asked Graeme.

"We already have a tree trunk in the middle now we had better get some order."

"I'm not as organised as you, am I, Graeme?"

"You're inclined to rush a bit, so go slowly. It will get done."

"Yes, I do get excited." So slowly they worked together, and the picture came to life.

"I think Lady Emily will like this," said Mark.

"I think so too, Mark," said Luke. The phone rang and Luke crossed his fingers before he answered."Hello, inspector, Luke here."

"We have the window safe and one person in custody plus the name of another, who is already on record. We'll soon pick him up," said the inspector.

"No damage?"

"None that we can see, Luke, but we shall need to hold for evidence."

"How long for do you think. It's a birthday present for an old lady, a surprise."

"When's her birthday," the inspector asked.

"Sometime in March," said Luke.

"Well, clarification is being sort."

"Right, let us know. If in situ somewhere it can be visited, but not actually produced and we will take photos."

"Just keep it safe, please, inspector, that's eight months of work you have there."

"That long!"

"Yes," replied Luke,"can you send someone to advise on security?"

"Certainly, will Monday morning at 10 am be suitable? Constable Young will come and advise you. Get your insurance company to send a representative, as they are fussy."

Luke pondered. He had deliberately been putting off insurance cover, as there was not a lot on money in the kitty at the moment. Reluctantly, he thought he may have to charge his students a small fee on a finished window. What could he do? He was struggling to pay the rent. Every start-up company had money problems unless they were cash rich to start off with. His business start-up, using the meagre savings he had, was obviously not enough. Still, as his old mum would say,"Every cloud has a silver lining, you just need to look for it."

"Yes, Mum, I can't see it at the moment."

The room was busy as everyone got on with their tasks, unaware of Luke's financial problems. Luke passed on the message from the inspector to Graeme. Graeme was pleased but disappointed at the same time, as he wanted his window back. Luke joined John and explained how he stood with his finances."Right," said John,"you knew there would come a time when you would have to charge. Let's work out some figures for new customers and/or second window production. I'll jot down my thoughts, but we are going to have to cost carefully. Not forgetting heating and lighting, telephone calls, teas and coffees. These are all costs to be considered."

"I don't like it, John, it leaves a bad taste in my mouth."

"Got to be done, Luke. You can't run on fresh air. Even your car needs petrol, oil and water plus servicing, not forgetting it's MOT!"

"Don't remind me, mine comes up at the end of the month."

"OK, I'll stay behind and do some costings, all right?"

"Thanks, John. You have a much better head for figures than me."

"You really need someone to back you as a shareholder."

"Then I would have to pay them," said Luke.

"You can pay them in kind and generate some publicity through the local newspaper, for example. That should bring in new custom." Luke thought this was a good idea.

"When Mark's window is ready, do you think we could invite the Lord Mayor and Lady Emily and any others we can think of?"

"It's a thought," said John,"you will need to talk to his family about it."

After everyone was gone, Luke took Mark home and made his way back to the workshop. He settled down with a cup of coffee and began to list categories. John let himself in, quietly, and saw Luke at his desk with his head in his hands."He's no business man," thought John. John was a caring, generous man and keen to help.

"Hello there, I'm back," said John."Now let's get started. Have you kept any finance figures?"

"Not really," replied Luke.

"OK, Luke, I hope your memory's good. What was the start-up finance available?"

"£5,000," said Luke.

"How much is the lease?"

"£125 per month for six months rising to £200 thereafter. I thought that wasn't too bad, but it soon mounts up."

"It's not exactly a palace, is it? Does that cover everything?"

"No," said Luke,"I have to pay for electricity used and water."

"Are these monitored separately for this building?"

"I don't know."

"I think they saw you coming! No more agreements without me being present, okay?"

"OK, John. Am I really that bad?"

"Unfortunately, there are a lot like you Luke starting up in business. A little bit naïve, not getting the proper advice and support. There are bound to be mistakes."

"Did the furniture come in with the price?"

"No, John, I bought that second-hand."

"How much?"

"I have the receipt here," and handed it to John.

"Good, that's a start. Do you have a copy of the lease?"

"Yes, this is the lease," and passed that over.

"Another thing, do you have receipts for all the materials you have bought?"

"Yes, I do, John."

"Splendid, Luke. I expect the blue glass is the most expensive?"

"Yes, it is."

"Well here is a sketch with numbers on, put a price to it." Luke looked worried.

"Now, we have to price:

1. A half-moon window
2. A half window
3. A full window as in the cathedral

"What a job, Luke. This should have all been done before you started."

"Yes, I so wanted to at the beginning."

"You will need an accountant to work on your figures. Especially as the tax man will soon want accounts from you."

"I can't afford an accountant, it's just someone else to pay."

"Leave it with me, Luke," said John,"I know just the man. He is retired at present, but restless for a small job no doubt."

"John, what would I do without you. You haven't had a salary ever either."

"All in good time. Maybe when the business is thriving."

"Do you think it will?"

"Indeed, it will, Luke, we just need to get sorted. How much money is left?"

"About a thousand pounds."

"That's good. You will need to open a bank account at the bank."

"I meant to do that, John, but never got around to it."

"Have we got enough figures to work out some prices?"

"Nearly there," said Luke.

"I will leave you with that task. Put all your receipts in this file for the accountant. He will be able to work much quicker than you. I will speak to him tomorrow. I think he will relish this job and present you with lots of ideas. Now let's tidy up and get home. I'll be in touch, Luke."

"Thank you so much, John, I feel a lot better already." They set about tidying up, turned everything off and left.

. . . .

The next day, a representative of the insurance company arrived, accompanied by Constable Young. It was a long meeting. Finally, an agreement was reached, and the representative said he would be in touch later. Luke questioned himself. Why hadn't he done this in the beginning? Better late than never, I suppose, he thought.

The following day, a Mr Shields came to visit Luke. He explained that it was he who had rang the police, as the stolen window had been offered to him."So glad I reported it, as I understand they have recovered the window." He then went on to say that he had a window that he thinks would look good with a stained glass design on it. He would like Luke to make it for him.

"Of course Mr Shields, but you do realise it is a long process and can take a number of months and there would be a fee. The exact price would be worked out once the design sketch was prepared. You can pay in instalments if you would find that easier and my accountant would handle that side of things."

"Yes, Luke, I'm in business myself so understand the process. Can I take a look around?"

So, Luke showed Mr Shields all of the work currently in progress."Very good work, Luke, we will get on just fine. I think I can put some business your way in the future."

"That would be much appreciated," said Luke,"but first, your window. Think about what you want on it and then I'll prepare a sketch to work from. Oh, and let me have the window measurements."

"Yes, of course. I will be in touch soon."

Luke took a box file from the shelf and wrote Mr Shields's name on it. He made a record of their conversation on paper, together with his business card and put them inside the file. Perhaps it will work after all. He would ask John to undertake the task."Our first paying project…but a wait before we get paid," said Luke to himself.

Pulling a clean sheet of paper towards him, he began to make a list of his student's names, in order of work. John would take Mr Shields's window. Graeme was next, as he had finished his. Charlie next, he was nearly finished and then, Mark, but he already had a second one to do. Nobody else was as advanced as these. Perhaps he would have to train more students if the business was to take off.

A knock at the door broke his train of thought."Hello there, do come in," said Luke. A grey head popped around the door.

"John asked me to call. I'm Mr Atkins, the accountant."

"Oh do come in," said Luke. A tall, neat figure emerged in the doorway, holding a briefcase.

"I've come to help."

"Thank you, I need it. Do sit down."

It wasn't long before they were deep into facts and figures. Luke was so relieved. By the end of the afternoon, they had made good progress and Luke was happy that it was all working out and becoming clearer. They began drawing up a plan of figures, to charge for various products. Mr Atkins, 'call me Jim' was very impressed by the work produced and pleased to hear of Mr Shields's new order. They parted at five o'clock, Jim leaving with a full briefcase of work and a very happy Luke. They agreed to meet again the following Wednesday. Luke packed up, locked up and left. He'd be back again tomorrow for the students.

. . . .

All students turned up as usual and Charlie brought a friend who wanted to learn the process. Charlie showed him around and Luke had a brief conversation, whilst waiting for John to arrive. When John arrived, Luke introduced him to Charlie's friend so John could vet him. Later, John reported back to Luke."He's keen enough but hasn't got the fee. I've told him what he needs and to come back when he has it. Don't hold out much hope, think he's a down and out."

"Couldn't we help him?" said Luke.

"No," said John,"we can't go down that road. You will lose any profits you may make, plus he'll probably tell his mates who will expect the same."

"I suppose so," said Luke. Charlie pleaded his friend's case and Luke left him to John to explain. Eventually, Charlie understood what was being said to him.

"We will try and help him," said Charlie,"but I really don't know him very well." He returned to his work and his friend left.

"John, a Mr Shields came to see me last week. He wants a full window done. Will you take it on?" asked Luke.

"With pleasure, Luke. Does he know the design he wants?"

"I think so. Here is his address, I have already asked for measurements. Can I leave this with you to sort?"

"You certainly can. A whole new window, my dream come true," said John.

"Did Jim Atkins come to visit you, Luke?"

"He did, yesterday. I think it's going to work out fine, thanks to you. Sorry I was such a green horn."

"We all can't know everything, Luke," said John."Do you need me for anything else? If not, I think I will take a visit to Mr Shields and introduce myself."

"You go. He will think we are very efficient!"

Everyone had left when John returned to the workshop.

"How did you get on?" asked Luke.

"Very well. He knew exactly what he wanted, and he didn't flinch when I mentioned an estimated cost."

"Good," said Luke,"that's progress."

"There's more. He introduced me to his neighbour, Mr Alsop, who wants a half moon window design to go over his door. He was very exact about what he wants, and he would like to visit when work is in progress."

"Well done, John. That's two paid jobs. I think Graeme should work on that one, what do you think?"

"I don't think Graeme would gel with Mr Alsop. He is very exact and straight to the point."

"Oh, dear, John, after you, Graeme is next in line to be given work. If not him who would be best suited do you think? Mark or Charlie."

"It would have to be Charlie as Mark has a second window to do."

"You will have to do the sketch, Luke. Charlie is not brilliant at the artwork."

"Are you sure Graeme won't do, John?"

"I think he lacks confidence," replied John.

"That is probably because of the affect the robbery has had on him. He has been helping Mark and to me, he is very competent and should be next in line. Let him do the sketch. Have you the details?"

"Yes, I have. I'll make up the files. I'll give Graeme my rough sketch and ask him to perfect it. Then we can take it from there. Sooner or later, he will have to work with a customer," said John.

"You're right. Let's give him a chance, we might be surprised."

After making up the two new customer files, including all details, John showed Luke his two rough sketches."These are good, John, not so rough either."

"Thanks, Luke."

"Well, I'll see you next week, John."

"I might come in on Wednesday when Jim is here. Would that be alright?"

"Alright, see you on Wednesday." John left. Luke settled down to review the two sketches. He thought he would speak to Jim regarding pricing the jobs accurately. He locked everything away, put out the burner and lights. He left, locking the door behind him.

"That's another thing," he thought,"new locks need to be fitted. A fire extinguisher needs installing too, according to the police report. All money to spend and no income as yet. Still, it's in the pipeline."

. . . .

Next morning at breakfast, Mark was eagerly telling his parents about his window and how it was nearly finished."Lovely," said Mum,"but you must show Lady Emily, like you promised. I thought you were inviting her and Gran to the fixing day?"

"Yes, we are, and the Lord Mayor."

"Gosh, what a day it will be!"

"We are just waiting to have it brought here so that we can arrange with John a convenient time to fit it. The invitations can then go out and when it's finally finished, I'll bring it home."

"I'm so excited to see it, Mark!"

"So am I, Mum. To think I have made it after all these months."

"Has Dad started his book yet?"

"It's all in his head at the moment, but, I don't think he will be long in starting."

"It's all happening, Mum, isn't it?"

"Yes. All because you asked questions and Gran tried to answer them. Keep asking questions, Mark, see where it leads you."

"I will, Mum, but I think we have more than enough on the go at present!"

"True."

"Now, I have Gran's window to do."

"Luke is coming today to see your dad and talk family trees."

"Is he, they should enjoy that."

"Yes, and I'm disappearing to your grans to make curtains."

"OK, Mum, I need to look for a silver birch tree to study its markings. See you at tea." His mother smiled as she left. All her family were happily occupied with their own projects, including her.

....

Luke knocked on the door and pushed it open."Can I come in?"

"Of course you can, nice to see you again. I understand our window is nearly finished?" said Dad.

"Yes, it is. Mark has done a good job."

"What do we owe you, Luke? We can't accept it for free. All those materials used have to be paid for. Even if we made a donation, we would feel better about it. After all, every business has to pay its way."

"A donation would be very acceptable," said Luke.

"What about Grandma's?" asked Dad.

"I'm afraid I will have to charge for a second one too."

"Quite right too. Let me know how much it will be. I might buy it for her new house, as a present."

"Please don't tell her, will you."

"No, I will leave that to you."

"Come into the next room. I will show you our family tree, it's rather long now."

"Is it finished?"

"Good gracious no," said Dad,"I am only back to the 1700s. I hope to get further back than that."

"It's a lot of work," said Luke.

"Yes, but very rewarding."

"Has it taken a lot of your time?"

"It has, Luke, but then I'm retired so have it to spare." They poured over the details and Luke asked a lot of questions."Don't worry, if you start yours and if I'm still around, I will help you."

"Thank you, that's very kind."

"I hope you will attend the fitting of our window, Luke. I am going to ask the Lord Mayor and of course, Lady Emily and Gran. Would John be able to fit it for us?"

"Of course, I'll come. Have you a date yet?"

"Not yet, we are waiting on Mark. He says he is nearly finished."

"Yes, he is," replied Luke.

They had a pot of tea and cake that had been left cut into slices for them and chatted."I will give Mark a cheque in an envelope for you to bring on Thursday, if that will be alright."

"Yes, fine. That's very good of you."

"Have you any more work coming in?"

"Yes, two more commissions as a result of the theft," replied Luke.

"That's interesting."

"Yes. Very unexpected."

"Do you have enough workers?" asked Dad.

"So far, yes."

"Well, I can say, Mark is thoroughly enjoying his work."

"That's good, I wouldn't want to lose him."

"No danger of that."

"Thanks for the information. I have enjoyed the afternoon, but I must leave now," said Luke.

"Thank you for coming Luke. Will let you know when the window is to be fitted, although I'm sure John or Mark will tell you."

"I'll find out and will be pleased to come."

They all sat around the tea table and exchanged news of their day."Luke says he will come to the window fitting. Would you ask John to fit it for us, Mark?" said Dad.

"Of course, Dad. About another ten days I reckon."

"Oh, lovely," said Mum."so much to look forward to."

"How did you get on, Mum?"

"Splendidly. We only have one room without curtains now and we got lots of other things done."

"Did you find your birch tree, Mark?" asked Mum.

"Yes, I did. It was near to the old windmill. A good specimen of a tree."

"Is this for our window?"

"Yes, it is – the finishing touches."

They spent the evening looking at the entries for the seventeenth century on the family tree."Dad, you have done a far better job of this than I ever could," said Mark.

"Perhaps I have had more time. You couldn't have done the research for the window and the family tree at the same time. It would have been too much work."

"I suppose so," agreed Mark.

"I think it's time we went to bed, don't you?" said Mum, yawning.

"Yes, Mum. You look tired."

"It's all the concentration!" Mark and his dad agreed.

. . . .

The following Thursday, Mark was given an envelope to give to Luke by his dad. His dad said it was the official invitation to the fitting of the window."Thank you," said Mark.

"Don't forget to ask John if he can fit it, will you?"

"I won't, Dad. He's here now, you ask him."

"John, could you find the time to fit Mark's window for us and let us have the costings?"

"I'm sure I can fit it in," replied John."When is it to be Mark?" John asked, as they got into the car.

"I don't know yet, John. I've still got the finishing touches to do. We will have to come up with a date soon as Dad wants the mayor to come."

"Goodness, quite a do then."

"Mum's in her element."

"I bet. The ladies like a party! A good excuse for a new outfit or a new hat." They both laughed.

On arrival at the workshop, Luke was talking to Graeme. Graeme looked pleased."Perhaps his window has been returned?" said Mark.

"I don't think so," said John. John joined Luke and Graeme just as Luke was handing over the sketch.

"Thanks for thinking of me. I will do my very best," said Graeme, as John and Luke exchanged a smile.

"Good lad," said John.

"I did the sketch if you have any questions."

"It looks straight forward," said Graeme,"but perhaps we could discuss colours later?"

"Yes, of course."

John turned to Mark."Need any help?"

"I will have to make that tree look like a silver birch."

"Count me out, Mark, ask Luke to help."

"Yes, I will." Mark picked up the envelope and went to Luke's desk. He handed the envelope over and Luke put it in his desk drawer.

"Are you not going to open it?"

"Yes, later. I know what it is, Mark. Your dad and I have already discussed it and I think you need my help, do you not?"

"Yes, I do. Could you show me how to apply the white paint needed on the birch tree and the colours to use on the stonework please?"

"Yes, have you found the paint yet?"

"No," said Mark.

"Let's be about it then," said Luke, making his way to the cupboard."We will start with the white. Can you fetch some clean brushes and a rag."

They settled down at Mark's workstation and Luke showed him how to turn the plain trunk into a silver birch tree."There now, got the idea now, so continue on to the finish, Mark, while I fetch the other paint." Mark, with some trepidation, picked up the brush and added another stroke."That's it, don't be afraid of it," said Luke, returning with more colours. Slowly, Mark gained confidence and soon began to see the difference in the stonework and the birch tree.

"That's much better, Luke. It makes all the difference, doesn't it?"

"Yes, so carry on then, Mark." Luke returned to his desk.

A knock at the door revealed Mr Alsop."I hope it's OK if I come in. My wife is that excited, I've got to report back." Luke took him over to Graeme. He took a chair over for him to sit down.

"Mr Alsop, this is Graeme who will be making your window."

"Hello, Graeme, have you produced one before?"

"Yes, Mr Alsop. It was the one that was stolen."

"I saw that one, it was good. So what happens now?"

"Well, this is the sketch of how you wanted your window to look. Are you happy with it?" asked Graeme.

"Yes, it looks better with the colours added."

"Now we have to decide on the exact colours in glass. Here is a list of colours to choose from. Looking at the sketch, there are three areas that are coloured green. Choose from the colour list which green you want where," said Graeme.

"You are not colour blind, are you, Mr Alsop?" asked Luke.

"Me, no. I'm not colour blind. Let me see now," said Mr Alsop, picking up the list.

"This one first," said Graeme, pointing at a specific area.

"I think this one."

"What is the number beside it?" He donned his reading glasses.

"That one is number 79." Graeme carefully wrote down his first choice.

"And this one." Mr Alsop peered at it, then back to the list."Number 73, that should do." He watched as Graeme noted down the colour.

"And the last one, number 75."

"That's the greens done. Now look at the corn stubble and the colours on the list."

"Number 55," said Mr Alsop, triumphantly.

"Mr Alsop, is this an autumn picture?" asked Graeme.

"Yes, it is."

"Then you must tell me what trees there are here, as they will be dressed for autumn and the leaves will no longer be green."

"That's a thought, Graeme. I have got some photos I took last autumn. Can you work from these?"

"I'll let you know when you bring them in."

"Now, what about the sky colour. Bearing in mind it's an autumn scene and not high summer."

"You really go into great detail, Graeme, don't you?"

"Yes, it must be right."

"Would number 16 be about right, do you think?"

"A good choice I think Mr Alsop," said Graeme.

"Now this plant in the foreground. What is it and what colour were those nearly dead flowers?"

"Pink, I think."

"Are we done for now?" said Mr Alsop.

"Just about."

Luke came over bringing the new window and the list of glass colours to give to John."It's nearly time to pack up. Thank you for helping out Graeme, Mr Alsop."

"My pleasure. He is very thorough."

"He will do a good job for you," said Luke.

"I'm sure he will," rising to his feet."Goodnight everyone," and he left.

"Well done, Graeme. He's not the easiest of customers, but you managed him very well."

John and Luke exchanged a nod, as Graeme sank back into his chair."Is he going to come every week?"

"I hope not," said Luke."We shall have to wait and see. He wasn't invited this time. He just turned up." Finally, they all packed up and locked things away.

"You were right, Luke," said Mark.

"Yes, I'm glad it worked out for you. Come on then, Mark, time to go home," said John. They left together. As they drove home, Mark asked John when he was free to fit his window.

"Is next week too soon?" asked John.

"Not for me, but Mum wants the mayor to attend and still needs to send an invitation. Which is why we need a date."

"I see. I'm fairly free next week, so see which day is best for the mayor and let me know."

"Thanks, John."

"By the way, Mark, I think your window looks grand. Are you pleased with it?"

"Yes, I am. Very pleased. I never ever thought I could do something like this."

"You never know until you try, Mark."

"Thanks for taking me initially and then every week thereafter, John."

"No trouble. Good night, Mark."

"Goodnight, John."

As Mark entered the house he met his mother."John said any day next week would be fine, Mum. He would fit in with the mayor. Will you invite Jeffrey?"

"From the cathedral? Yes, of course I will. Your dad has already invited Luke. So, you can tell him the date and time, or we can ring him."

"It's getting close, Mum. I thought I would never finish it, but now it's done. I think I'll go off to bed now, do you mind?"

"Not at all my son. We are very proud of you," and then she pulled him to her, giving him a big hug.

"Thanks, Mum," said Mark, taking a big gulp and so, that day ended.

Lying in bed, he went over all that had happened and the people that had helped him. So many. He was lucky and now he had Grandma's to start. Lovely!

. . . .

Next morning at breakfast, Dad said he was going to invite the local newspaper."Not yet. We don't have a date," said Mum.

"They will know what the mayor is doing."

"I suppose so," said Mum.

"Will I have my name in the paper?" asked Mark.

"I expect so. Your dad's on the phone to the mayor's office now. We might get a date from them." Dad came off the phone."Any luck dear?"

"Oh yes, as soon as I mentioned newspapers, things started happening. I was asked 'Can he bring his wife.' I said of course, and the date is…!"

"Dad, stop holding us in suspense."

Laughing, his dad said,"Next Tuesday at 2 pm."

"At last, I can go ahead and make arrangements," said Mum.

"Not quite yet," said Dad.

"What now?"

"I want to ring the newspaper first."

"Go on then," said Mum.

"You are like a couple of kids!" said Mark, laughing.

"We are both so excited for you, of course," said Mum.

"Of course," grinned Mark."I'll leave you both to it."

Getting on his bike, Mark went for a ride. On his return, everything had settled down and his mum was on the phone.

"Who is Mum talking to, Dad?"

"Jeffrey," replied Dad.

"Good, we must not forget him."

"Now we won't see Mum for days."

"Why?"

"Well, because people will be visiting and there's baking to be done. There is sure to be a special cake and your gran won't be left out either, you'll see," said Dad.

"I expect you're right, Dad. Where shall we go? Is there a good film on?" said Mark, laughing.

"Cheeky. Let's find out."

"Roll on, Tuesday."